GOT 8 IF YOU WANT 'EM

The First Short Story Collection by

BULL MARQUETTE

BRAVE NEW GENRE, INC.

Fresno, CA

BRAVE NEW GENRE, INC.
Publishers of Books, Music & Films
6535 N Palm Ave. #101
Fresno, CA 93704
www.bravenewgenre.com

Library of Congress Control Number: 2008943089

Marquette, Bull
Got 8 If You Want 'Em/Bull Marquette
ISBN 978-0-9820474-1-5

1. Fiction 2. Short Stories
3. Paranormal—Fiction 4. Science Fiction
5. Mysteries 6. Slapstick

Also by Bull Marquette:

THE FIFTH PLANE --a novel, a paranormal thriller of an alternate history that tells what happened to the hero of a mythical ""fifth" plane on 9/11 – where the passengers revolted, like those brave souls on Flight 93 – but this time, they won.

Order <u>THE FIFTH PLANE</u> *and/or* <u>GOT 8 IF YOU WANT</u> *'EM on the Web on any of these websites:*
www.bravenewgenre.com (and check this one for more publications and products as they are released), or:
http://www.createspace.com/3353118 , or:
http://www.amazon.com/ .

Communicate with the publisher, or Bull Marquette at:
info@bravenewgenre.com.

Print-On-Demand, first release: February, 2009.
Cover art © 2009 by Marshall Patrick Smith.

For Laurie –
with thanks for all the time you gave me to write.

The Stories:

Under A Nyuk-Y Star*
By Bull Marquette
    *First featured on the radio program,
    Valley Writers Read on KVPR-FM, Valley
    Public Radio, on April 7, 2006.

Barkonet fidgeted on the marble bench, gazing through the window at the clashing afternoon shadows generated by two of the Castor system's six great stars. How nice it would be to stroll on those faraway grassy knolls, sit under a terrabounce tree, and run his eighteen fingers through the hair of Dr. Seville, the most attractive female member of Dr. Rugo's verification committee. Oops. He sat up straight. Such a lapse of attention could be dangerous.

"Ah-hmm." Dr. Rugo cleared his throat, pacing alongside the great marble table atop the stage.

The old fraud is prancing, Barkonet thought. I brought him the radio astronomy find of the century, and he's trying to figure out a way to cop the credit.

At last the scrawny academic halted and the committee members sat upright, arranging their papers in unison. Seville's back was to Barkonet. So lovely. Even from behind.

"Approach." Rugo sank ceremoniously into his throne. The members posed in stony silence.

"You have discovered an interesting alien race in these television signals, Astronomer Barkonet. But you are wrong about the odd sounds these creatures emit. It is simply a guttural wheeze. Disgusting, actually. Evidence of disease. Their race will be extinct soon, perhaps already is."

Around the table, heads nodded, except for Dr. Vicking, the show-boater, who began to whine. "Astronomer Barkonet, these television transmissions were discovered by accident?"

"Yes, sir, I--"

Vicking held up a wrinkled hand. "And their source is a star named *Sol*, some fifty light years distant?"

"Sol's third planet. The inhabitants call it *Earth*."

"Call it? They have a language, too?" Vicking scowled, even though that fact was firmly established on page one of the report. "Good Lord, could these monsters still be living?"

Steam might have been coming from Rugo's ears if it were fog season. He answered for Barkonet. "Of course not, Doctor. Can't you see?" He threw a switch and moving lithographs flashed on the stage's view screen.

"These--*animals*--are nothing more than a race of sickly, inferior demons. Just look. They have no third arm, for God's sake. How can they reach for their Creator at the moment of death? How can they pin their children down while whaling on them? Un-evolved. They certainly died out in the multi-years it took for these signals to reach us."

That's not the point, Barkonet wanted to scream, but did not.

Dr. Seville looked up from a small verifier. "Mr. Chairman," she said, "one aspect of our young protégé's hypothesis might be valid. The sounds these aliens make match exactly with records of our own people from before the Ancient Apocalypse. These creatures seem to be laugh--"

"Don't say it." Rugo waved all three of his arms frantically. "Your instrument has been known to mistake terminal coughing for the same thing. These unfortunate mutants are long dead." He stared down each professor in turn. The verdict was in.

"Your report is neat, Barkonet, and the way you put spaces between the paragraphs is intriguing. File these clips and report for a new assignment tomorrow morning. You will spend no more time on these *Earth-lings*." His snide pronunciation classed the far-away other-worlders somewhere below desert coal-worms.

The senior scholars returned Barkonet's bows as they filed out, eyes glazed over, any true opinions shrouded by poker faces. How many other great scientific revelations had been suppressed in this same manner?

No harm done, Barkonet thought. Dr. Rugo's compliments, however faint, would carry weight on his transcript. He was a cinch now for the doctoral track.

As ordered, he transmitted the recordings to the Academy Vault. Yet, only moments before the nightly sign-off, something possessed him, and he directed his office computer to do a quick survey: *Find the most consistent cause of laughter on this world called Earth, from the decade or so of available recorded signals, a period the Earthlings called 1938-1952.*

Seville knew, he was certain. Probably the others, too. Those Solarian Earth creatures were emitting *laughter*, a ritual outlawed throughout the civilized Castor System for these thousands of years.

He waited nervously while the machine whirred. Sweat dripped from his ears and he pretended to dampen a radiation stick, just in case the monitors were watching him over the purity cameras. The computer clanked and strained. What was he thinking? Some alien races were too hard for these rusty government processors to analyze. The damn thing would tilt, and security would review his program. He would be sent to the ice caves!

The machine sputtered. He could take it no longer. Admitting his error would result in a lighter sentence. He faced the camera, ready to confess directly into it, when reels of the distant television transmissions began to issue forth. He stuffed the illegal strips into his homework case and scurried toward the main gate.

He paced nervously in his room after dinner, barely able to wait until the brightest suns, Whitey, Greeny, and Yaller-Boy set. That left the two duller stars, the Orange Monkeys still in the sky. Blue-Bell would not rise for hours. Finally, enough dimness descended for the population to sleep. Barkonet drew the blinds, turned on the view screen, and threaded the first film with shaking fingers.

Moving pictures flickered to life. He sat, mesmerized, and half of the night burned away before he realized it.

Strange. Sometimes the odd *hiccupping* that must be laughter came directly from the creatures he watched moving on the screen. At other times, it seemed to ooze from the ether around the characters. Had an invisible audience been recorded and overlaid on the sound track? Why?

All the strips shared a common theme: three bizarre-looking characters were repeatedly the main protagonists. Even more mysterious, laughter occurred only when the three oddballs performed acts that were ridiculous or injurious, such as falling out of a building, or smashing one another in the face with a spanner.

An old Castorian saying contended, "Curiosity demolished a continent." Yet Barkonet could not help himself. As a scientist, he longed to understand how the crazy motions of those three loathsome buffoons on the barbaric records could cause laughter.

When he finally nodded off to sleep in the wee hours, the tapes inspired nightmares. In one, his dear departed mother hugged him--yet there between her breasts, where her third arm should be, was nothing but cleavage, *ala* the Earth women.

In another night horror, he walked into his father's study, only to discover the old man had shaved himself bald, like the tubby member of the alien laughter trio. That image shook Barkonet to his very soul when he woke, and he almost called the nursing home to ask if his dad was still on the "functioning" list.

"Focus on harmony," he reminded himself, while morning cleaning rods passed over his back. Such a call might alert the science police. What were the psychological implications of dreams that cast his own father as one of those three *stooges*--the Earth name for the films' hurtful instigators of the laughter spasm? My God. Barkonet stuffed the film strips up high in his closet, out of reach.

He threw himself with zest into the galactic transmissions of his new assignment, but the concentration wasn't there. His thoughts kept drifting back to those disgusting films.

Laughter was illegal. A just law on this world, but the Earthlings seemed to thrive on it. True, those stooges were forever being damaged from blows, pokes, and punches, yet rarely did they appear broken or bruised. Did physical injury protect them from hilarity's fatal effects?

"Hey, Barky," his friend Charleston called from his cubicle. "You're going to sleep over there. Keep your pipes tuned into those star-chirpings or we'll blow the whole experiment."

"Of course. Thought I heard an anomaly," Barkonet lied.

In the transport home, the taped images kept returning to his mind. Why did Earthlings laugh when a stooge poured tiny insects down the crude garment covering a party hostess's two-armed body? What was so comical about bonking each other on the head, or the frantic dance these stooges performed after gripping each others' noses and slapping downward in a motion which surely caused pain?

Exhausted, Barkonet collapsed into his bed without dining. He ordered himself not to lose any more sleep over these horrid alien tapes. A good Castorian scientist relied on the inner brain, that greatest of all computers. Answers to all his questions would come of their own accord. That's right – the solutions would come if he just let it go.

Sometime before dawn, though, he found himself in a vivid dream. Observatory staffers were attending the Lunar Day Picnic. He stood in the buffet line and heaped his wood-slab with sweet-meats, then headed for the large orange blanket set aside for the Distant Civilizations Recording Department.

As he prepared to feast, the antics of the alien stooge creatures stealthed from his memory. In one crystal instant, their bizarre machinations seemed … logical.

Deftly, his dream self, in a motion even Earth-beings might have appreciated, reached across, grasped a nearby bowl in both hands, and dumped a quart of pudding onto the head of frumpy Dr. Juno, the acknowledged witch of the department. His colleagues stared in alarm. Mouths fell open, third arms circled in the sign of the Redeemer…

Barkonet woke in a panic. The strangest bellowing guffaw pushed out of his throat.

"Haw-haw, hee-hee," he heard his voice echo through the domicile. His eyes watered. His heart felt so full it might burst. His lungs heaved.

A glance around was required to make sure his room had not switched to *weightless*, for his stomach tickled uncontrollably, as when falling off of a boozing table at a party. He strained to catch his breath, but the motions only worsened as he remembered the image of Madame Juno blubbering beneath her coating of dessert.

"My god, I'm laughing," Barkonet yelled into the darkness. Immediately, all three hands flew up to cover his mouth. Blasphemy!

A banging at the door. "Are you quite well?" The gravelly voice of Mrs. Valeinz, his landlady.

"Mmph," Barkonet called out, answering her, his face buried in his pillow. "Fine, ma'am. Just a nightmare."

After an excruciating spell, his belly quit heaving. Amazing. He felt so light, so alive, vibrating in every limb. Why in Castor-world had such an exhilarating experience been outlawed? Did the ancients fear it would lead to drug abuse?

His euphoria evaporated on the transport to work the next morning. The familiar workers' faces stared at him, quizzically, more attentive than usual to his every move. What if he were under surveillance? The science police possessed all sorts of secret gadgets the public had little knowledge of. What if they heard him laughing and recorded the whole episode somehow? God, why hadn't he turned on the video scanner this morning – his heresy might be all over the talk shows. Barkonet's cheeks burned. He wiped moisture from his ears and took deep breaths. Please, God, if he could only go to work, like normal, and not be found out, there would be no more blasphemy in the house of Barkonet.

His resolve held for most of the morning. In moments of weakness, however, replays of the stooges' pratfalls stole upon him, the smashing-faces-with-boards, the twanging arrows misdirected into Earthly butts (which the films showed were somewhat larger than the average Castorian ass).

Finally, he could stand it no longer, and did the unthinkable. He switched off the stream of signals coursing into his computer from distant galaxies and re-programmed it to scan the ancient law-making process which banished laughter from Castorian society so long ago.

The first entries, from Castor 1-5, were so old the auto-translator could barely decipher them. Speeches revealed that those were hard times. The population of the sixty-five planets which circled the six-sun Castor system grew hungry, rebellious. Jobs were scarce. As one legislator aptly put it, "What was there to laugh about?" Still, such arguments left something out.

Barkonet tweaked the scanner forward in time, reading heart-rending testimonies of citizens sentenced to die for laughing in the first centuries of *comic prohibition*. The accused criminals invariably described the same happy feelings, rushes of blood, smiles gone amuck, that Barkonet felt every night, watching the Earth-stooge chronicles.

"Barkonet, why is your scope un-tuned?" The worried voice belonged to Dr. Seville. She looked comely today, her Castorian drape falling lightly down her lithe body, exposing one shapely leg, the very definition of fashion. His gaze drifted to where her sensitive, poised arm protruded from between her breasts.

"*Hubba-hubba*," he said, quoting the stooges themselves. Her brow furrowed in puzzlement. He sputtered in panic, and tried to change the subject. "As you know, Doctor Seville, I applied to be your understudy. Has the chairman made assignments yet?"

"Not yet," she replied as he scrambled to set the scope right. She drifted away, down the laboratory aisle. Was that a faint smile? Barkonet sighed. He would do anything to win her favor.

As he half-listened to the scope's remote chirpings, a plan began to form. An outline every bit as preposterous as the goofy get-rich-quick schemes those stooges were always hatching.

Had the ancients been wrong? What if laughter were the very thing needed by a society so afraid and lethargic that it searched the heavens for new civilizations that might give them meaning? If so, and if Barkonet revealed such a momentous truth, Dr. Seville would have to notice him.

Yet such a broad hypothesis could not be fully drawn until he performed a trial experiment. *With Seville as the subject? No. Not yet, anyway.*

At home, streetlights were igniting while he set up his viewer, stacking galaxy abstracts beside it in case the science police staged a surprise inspection. A loud knock at the door jolted his being, and he stopped threading the first Solarian tape.

"Yes?"

The door opened. It was Charleston.

"Barkonet, old buddy. Come out and see the sunset. Don't tell me you forgot?"

Out on the lawn, the festivities had already begun. Once every three years all six suns of Castor, differently hued and brilliant, moved into conjunction and set at the same time. This holiest of days was today.

"I've seen it, and how," Barkonet replied testily, surprised to hear more stooge phraseology seeping into his speech.

Charleston stared wide-eyed. "What does that mean? Hurry or we'll miss the holy *Fall of Night.*"

Wait--his old friend was usually open-minded. Who better as the subject for the first experiment? Barkonet took a deep breath and stood. Now or never. He approached his puzzled friend.

"Nyuk-nyuk-nyuk," he said, and waved a hand slowly in front of Charlie's face. Back and forth. Up and down.

Charleston could not seem to help himself; he followed the motion with his head and eyes, just like a stooge would. Barkonet finished the ritual by raising his hand high, then slamming it straight down. Charleston jerked toward the floor in one violent nod.

"Ow! My God, my neck's sprained. That hurt."

"You mean, that *hoit*." Barkonet adapted the stooge pronunciation. He held up the fingers of one hand. "Pick two," he commanded.

"Uh?" Charleston stared, dumbfounded for a moment, then glanced over at the view-scope. "Oh, I get it. You're researching an alien procedure. What fun."

"Pick two," Barkonet repeated, relieved that his friend was so perceptive.

Charleston studied the fingers. "All right," he said with a smile, but made no movement.

"Why you lamebrain." The stoogish insult burst out, and Barkonet could not resist slapping the Charleston noggin. "It's not a telepathy test. Pick two *fingers*. Indicate them by touching them."

Shyly, his lifelong buddy obeyed, pinching two near the middle. In one swift move, rehearsed in the dark many times last night, Barkonet jammed the chosen digits into Charlie's eyes.

"My god." His friend screamed, dancing in pain. "What strange customs are you duplicating? You bastard, I'll tell the Council."

"Wait," Barkonet cried as the writhing scientist hurtled out onto the crowded lawn. "You're supposed to bark or look cross-eyed." But Charleston was gone.

Barkonet sank forlornly into his chair. Perhaps Castorians were not ready. Slowly, the stunned look on Charlie's face came back to him. A small laugh – was that what the ancients called a "chuckle?" – rose from his esophagus. "What a knucklehead," he muttered, quoting the stooge with straight black hair.

Paranoia returned. At the lab the next day, Charleston was mysteriously absent, supposedly temporarily re-assigned to another department. Sweat soaked Barkonet's three armpits. He had read that a favorite ploy of the science police was to move their informant out, away from the suspect under surveillance, then replace him with a trained spy. Yet, no one took Charlie's place. More than a week passed before anything unusual occurred.

"Barkonet, you are wanted in Rugo's office," Ms. Alpheratz said quietly, one afternoon. Why was she smiling? This must be a trick.

"Why me, toots? What gives, anyway?" he spouted without thinking.

"He's handing out understudy assignments. Weren't you waiting for one?"

Barkonet trudged down the long halls, passing several exits along the way. Why not take it on the lam? That's what the stooges did in the army episode, when they accidentally hit their sergeant in the butt with a saber. Yet, he stayed the course and, happily, Dr. Seville was also waiting in Rugo's palatial office.

"You wished to see me, sir?"

"Astronomer Barkonet." Rugo sneered. "You will prepare an exhibition sketch on the galactic emission patterns you have been studying. I want you to present it at the upcoming Planetary Science Convention."

Barkonet whipped out his burned wood and papyrus to scribble down the format the old man required for his speech. What an honor. Plus, exposure in front of billions of the greatest brains from all over the

Castorian realm. Dr. Seville winked in approval as he
scraped out the instructions in charcoal.

"To conclude, Astronomer Barkonet--" A cloud
seemed to cross Rugo's countenance. "--Dr. Seville is here
because I had planned to appoint her as your mentor for
the upcoming multi-year."

"Wonderful." Barkonet bowed. Seville sat
demurely, her hair pulled back, radiantly sexy. "Uh--*had*
planned?"

"Yes. I'm afraid we received a rather nasty report
from Astronomer Charleston about your behavior. He
seems to think you have been studying alien cultures too
intently."

"Oh, no, sir--"

"Before you answer, I would like you to hear
something." Rugo extracted a player from his desk and
punched the button. Quietly at first, then so loud it
required muffling, the unmistakable hearty guffaws of
Barkonet himself resounded through the office.

He felt blood rise to his cheeks. They had bugged
his room. Seville looked concerned.

"Do you have an explanation for this recording,
Astronomer?"

"Think fast," the voice of the dark-haired stooge
popped into his brain. That tower of strength would be
equal to this situation. He would sort out old Rugo with
a swift kick. Barkonet sighed. Castorians were no match
for such quick wits, thus, he could only lie, partially.

"Sir, that is a recording of one of the Earth
transmissions. I abrogated the rules, Mr. Chairman, and

took a tape home. They were so fascinating. I apologize officially."

"I see," Rugo announced after a long pause. "Just as I feared. You will destroy the offending tape as soon as you return home?"

Barkonet met the cold eyes. "*Coitainly,*" he said.

He waited for the elevator, quaking, never believing Rugo would let a breach of this magnitude go so easily, sure that every footfall down the hall must be the cops. Dr. Seville emerged. *Straighten up, it's the dame,* a voice echoed in his brain. The stooges would never let a female see them nervous.

"Hey sugar, I can explain--" he started, mimicking the pudgy one's sheepish plea to his wife in one episode where the stooges were caught drinking liquor.

Seville refused eye contact, though her cheeks colored. "I have just one question, Barkonet," she said evenly. "I can forgive you if you prevaricated under these circumstances, but wasn't that actually your voice, and not that of the Earthlings on the tape?"

A high pitched alarm announced the elevator's approach. *Trapped like a rat,* the voice of the black-haired stooge almost came out of the ether.

"You got me, dead to rights, toots." Barkonet winked, amazed at how freely stooge-talk flowed now. "Say, you're not a stool pigeon, are ya?"

She whipped around and glared searchingly with those enchanting blue-speckled eyes. "What is it like to laugh?" she asked.

He did a double-take, and his body seemed to know what to do next. He reached toward her with the fingers of his third hand, while his side hands rose to fluff his hair, in the fashion of the skinny stooge.

"Baby," he said, and chucked her under the chin, "I could go for you in a big way. Nyuk-nyuk-nyuk."

She stared, wide-eyed. A spark of electricity passed between them, he felt sure of it. He leaned closer. "Ruff, ruff," he mimicked, leaning close enough to bite her.

Instantly, Seville's right hand flew up and slapped him. Hard. Then she stepped back and stared at the appendage, obviously startled by her own behavior.

"Hey," Barkonet said in the high tenor of the tubby stooge, "that's exactly what the Earth girls do. I'm tantalized." The elevator opened and crowding bodies separated them. When he finally pushed through, Dr. Seville was nowhere to be seen.

The evening lagged. Guilt, embarrassment, terror, despair, the worst demons that prey on Castorian psyches swirled in packs through his head.

Had he made a fool of himself? She knew. If only she would come over and study the tapes with him. Perhaps she would perceive – as he had – how laughter could add to the discourse between a man and woman. Didn't the stooges seem deliriously happy, cavorting and laughing with their women, up until the moment those same ladies threw furniture or shot at them with guns?

Next morning, he called her on the videophone. The answer-robot announced she was occupied, preparing her own paper for the Convention. Damn. He checked his mail. No arrest warrants. At least she had not *ratted* on him, as the stooges would say.

How he longed to laugh with her, hand-in-hand, gliding through intoxicating forests of *smoke cane*. They could cavort at a fueling station, spray water and oil into customers' faces, slap each other, and pinch each other's noses until those patrons were forced to cackle at such hilarious antics. My God, laughter might become an integral part of an entire new form of mating ritual.

Why should laughter be criminal? Somehow, the trusted academics of Castor had helped to deprive hundreds of generations of a wonderful gift. Why hadn't great brains like Rugo's uncovered the mistake? Maybe they had.

"Those lamebrains need some new brains," Barkonet dared to utter into the stuffiness of his cramped cubicle. How to enlighten them? At least Seville?

On his day off, instead of taking the air along the canals, he paced in his room, hatching scheme after scheme, just as the stooges would. The trial run with Charleston had been all wrong. When Earthlings laughed, it was not one person, but many. The Convention would be a better venue. Yes, if one laughed, the authorities could quash it. If billions laughed, Barkonet's findings would stand forever, and Seville would be his.

Four suns smudged the sky on the morning of the Convention. Barkonet mounted the steps toward the great stone stage. The droning voice of the first presenter boomed through loudspeakers over the teeming mass of four billion scientists in the Great Concourse below.

A murmur went through the crowd as Barkonet took his seat among the dignitaries behind the rostrum. Dr. Rugo did a double-take, apparently horrified by Barkonet's bald head, newly shaved in honor of the tubby stooge. Barky waved his hand in dismissal and uttered a stoogey "Ehhh."

Mentally, he rehearsed his speech. His usual stage fright had disappeared. "Without laughter, there is no courage," one of the ancients had claimed during the banishment debates. Now that he could laugh, would he always have courage?

When Barkonet's turn came, Dr. Rugo seemed to think twice about even introducing him, but relented, and wheezed into the microphone, "Astronomer Barkonet will speak on emission analyses of seventy nearby planetary systems." His eyes teemed with suspicion.

"Nyuk-nyuk," Barkonet whispered as he passed him. "Thanks, Pops."

"Fellow scientists, citizens of Castor 3-12, and assorted idiots," he began. Thoughts of the stooges, the way they carried themselves, their quick, sure actions flooded his mind. This was right. This would work. He glanced at Seville over his shoulder, twiddled his fingers at her, and smiled.

In a loud voice, Barkonet began to sing, "B-A-Bay," and proceeded through the strange stooge anthem which featured word plays using the Earthly alphabet.

Puzzled conventioneers were spell-bound. Barkonet glared down at them when the first stanza ended. The auto-translators deciphered the alien tongue perfectly, yet these goons just stood there.

"You numbskulls ain't got it," he admonished. "When I stop, you're supposed to sing, *Barkonet's a dope.* Give it a try."

With little energy, a few voices parroted the phrase.

"Oh, I perceive," Professor Trundle interrupted from the side of the stage. "An interactive speech. Remarkable. We haven't seen this in fifty multi-years. Should be educational." A rumble coursed through the vast audience. Rugo seethed.

"That's better," Barkonet crowed. "Nyuk-nyuk. Thanks, Prof." He saluted the old geezer, then used a finger to make a *popping* noise with his mouth. "Now, take it from the top. B-I-bickey-bye--"

At the end of the verse, billions of voices, singing in perfect pitch, drowned out the loudspeakers. "Barkonet's-a-dope," they thundered.

"Poi-fect," he yelled in triumph, then twirled around and advanced on the seated Dr. Juno. Startled, she did not resist when he pinched her ear and dragged her center-stage.

"Ow-wow-wow-wow," she wailed.

He reached for the water pitcher under the podium and smashed it over her head.

"Woo-woo-woo," he crowed, then scrambled toward Professor Trundle, and snatched out handfuls of gray hair.

"Yow," Trundle screamed.

Barkonet produced a fist. "Hit that." Trundle did, sending the fist down, then up in a big arc, until it bopped the top of the professor's head.

"Oooh!"

"Here, now." Dr. Scog tapped Barkonet's shoulder from behind. "Stop this nonsense."

"What nonsense, you four-flusher?" He spun Scog around, grasped his suspenders, pulled back and released. The twanging *snap* reverberated through the speakers.

"Gaah!" Scog sailed forward, propelled by the elastic force toward the middle of the stage bleachers. He landed, collapsing them, and sending scientists flying in every direction.

"Woo-woo-woo," Barkonet wailed. He ran in place with arms and legs flailing while dazed profs crowded the stage exit. But what was that noise? Far below and to the left, a choppy sound wafted over the heads of the teeming crowd. Barkonet leaned over the podium.

There, in the middle of a widening circle left by the retreating audience, a lone woman stood, stooped over, seized by horrendous convulsions. The sound bounced off the tall buildings and finally caught up with the vision he was witnessing: she was laughing!

Then, on the other side of the Concourse, two men fell to the ground, cackling as loudly as any guest at one of the garden parties the stooges always crashed on the film strips. Like an ice-river cratering under the force of stun darts, many more spaces opened up in the sea of Castorian bodies. At the center of each clearing, someone laughed.

"Nyuk-nyuk-nyuk," Barkonet called into the microphone. "That's more like it." He rubbed his bristly scalp, then brought his hands down over his face in short, repeated motions. "Ruff. Ruff," he said.

Suddenly, the air crackled with lightning. Two loud blasts. Three. Four claps of thunder. A deafening chorus of screams. The crowd bolted and ran. Ten--twenty surgical knives of electricity jabbed down from a silver ship hovering above. In seconds, those who had dared to laugh were transformed into smoking carcasses on the tarmac. Onstage, frantic professors crashed together, heading for the exits.

Dr. Rugo elbowed in front of Barkonet and grabbed the mike. "Be calm, friends," he yelled, and the towering buildings turned his voice into an echoing chorus of stuffed shirt academics. "The danger is past," he cried, rapping his gavel. "Have no fear. Our colleague, Barkonet, has participated in a police plan to uncover hidden laughers. The criminals are vanquished. Three cheers for brave Barkonet."

The crowd responded with gusto and a great hurrah shook the same buildings which moments before had played host to a happy sound unheard here these thousands of years. Grappling hands hustled Barkonet backstage. A dozen policemen surrounded him, and only parted to make way for Rugo, himself.

"You are finished, Astronomer," he said with a hiss. Dr. Seville, all the more beautiful for her mussed hair and torn dress, stood to the side, wiping away tears.

Barkonet protested, "Dr. Rugo, they were laughing. They felt real happiness for once in their lives.

Why kill them for it? If you were so displeased, why did you protect my reputation out there?"

"I protected the reputation of the Academy. We must maintain our ranking above the Plumber's Union. You will be disposed of, but discretely, because you are an unsalvageable idiot."

The word *idiot* touched a nerve.

"Woo-woo-woo," Barkonet howled, did a little dance, and kicked Rugo in the pants.

"Seize him."

The guards rushed forward again. Barkonet's hands flew up automatically.

"Spread out," he ordered, as powerfully as the black-haired stooge ever did. The startled guards shuffled back, then followed those dodging hands, side-to-side, up--up. He swooped them down violently, and the nodding cops went tumbling to the floor.

"That'll *loin* ya'," Barkonet crowed.

"I'll take care of this." Charleston, his clothes rumpled from the melee, plunged forward and held up six fingers. "Pick two," he commanded.

Barkonet's eyes met his opponent's. In a motion born of intense practice, he chose two digits, then deftly lodged his own middle hand flush to his nose, blocking Charleston's attempt at the patented poke-in-the-eyes.

He lifted another hand to Charlie's eye-level, and wavered it--up, down. *Pop-pop-pop*, he boxed the stunned man's forehead.

As Charleston staggered, Barkonet sprawled to the floor on his side, ran with his feet, propelling his body around in circles, knocking guards every which way. "Woo-woo-woo," he cried.

"He's a menace."

The guards recovered, pinned Barkonet, then shoved him into the convention hall's heat-execution canister.

"There." Rugo gloated as they strapped him in. "We'll see how funny you think this is."

"What's the big idea?" Barkonet found the Earth phrase more to-the-point than any Castorian saying.

"You fool." Rugo leered. "Laughter was expunged for a reason. Did it ever occur to you what would happen if the thirty trillion souls on the sixty-five planets of our beloved system were allowed to laugh? Mayhem. Sheer mayhem.

"Laughter is a disease," he lectured, his breath fogging the Plexiglas death capsule. "Our ancestors proved that. If everyone carried on like you did up there, billions of people would die yearly. At least you did us the service of exposing several laughing renegades."

Barkonet's stomach fell away. Could Rugo be correct? He sought Seville's eyes, but she only gazed downward and blushed.

"Still, there is a greater thing you accomplished." Rugo swelled to his task. "You answered a question which worried us since the dawn of the first radio telescope."

"Oh, yeah? What's that, *wisenheimer*?"

Rugo did a double-take, then recovered. "You solved the Great Postulate: Can disease be transmitted intergalactically via radio and television waves? You proved it can be. Barkonet, my son, your name will live forever in the halls of science. We will disassemble our radio telescope program tomorrow morning. No more watching for alien communications. They are hazardous to our health." He turned. "Come, colleagues, let the security detail do their job."

The professors and most of the cops followed Rugo while the two guards nearby secured the heavy see-through lid. Barkonet knew how these things worked: once sealed, the capsule--with him in it--would jet downwards into the volcanic incinerator below the city.

"Wait." Dr. Seville held up her hand. "He's a scientist and must answer the ritual debriefing questions about his classified projects."

Rugo paused, frowning. "I'm not aware of any classified assignments we give to Astronomers 2nd Class, but very well." He resumed walking.

Seville approached cautiously, a nervous look on her face. "Please?" she said to the two remaining guards. They both shrugged and retreated into a corner.

Barkonet struggled vainly against his bindings. How ironic. He felt himself thinking in crisp scientist's logic for the first time in weeks, yet Seville looked more alluring than ever, even at a time like this.

"I'm sorry this happened, Barkonet," she said in her gloriously textured voice, "but I need to ask you--"

"I don't have any classified projects," he whispered through the air vents that were yet open.

"I know."

"Dr. Seville, I've failed the Academy--and you. If the chairman is correct, I may be a threat to our planet's mental health. God save me if I started some evil epidemic. Can you forgive me?"

Seville stared at him. Was she, the queen of Academia, actually panting? She turned the handle, and raised the canopy, admitting fresh air and her lyrical voice. "Did you mean what you said before?"

"What? When?"

She leaned close. "That you could, how did you say it--*go for me in a big way?*"

Barkonet felt his jaw drop. She leaned inside, her lips touching his ear. "Can you teach me to laugh?"

"Laugh?" My God, what was she doing?

With a loud click, she flipped the release lever. The straps gave way and he fell forward and out, knocking her down in the process.

"Hey, you can't do that," someone bellowed. Both guards rushed for them.

Seville pulled him up, her face frightened, but radiant.

"Quick. What do we do first?" she asked.

Heart pounding, Barkonet had no idea. Through the fog, he heard the voice of the dark-haired stooge. "Am-scray, lame-brain, am-scray."

Barkonet motioned. "Tell him to pick two--" Seville wheeled to face the fat one.

The taller guard loomed over them, his stun truncheon drawn. Barkonet held up a fist.

"Hit that," he commanded, at the very moment that Seville cried out,

"Pick two."

The startled guards did as told, and while Barkonet's fist was smashed, and flew down, then up in its arc, her chosen fingers found their way into the shorter guard's eyes. Barkonet's fist hit the tall one's skull, and both cops went crumpling to the floor.

The astronomer gave Seville a wink. "Now you're cooking with gas," he said. "Nyuk-nyuk."

"Nyuk-nyuk," she answered gaily.

"Let's high-tail it."

They raced out the back corridor, just as reinforcements appeared at the far opening.

"In here," he directed. They jumped into an elevator and punched for the parking deck. It whined downward.

"If they catch us, we'll be *murdalized*. But don't worry, toots, I know just the speakeasy to hole up in until the heat's off. Nyuk-nyuk." He twiddled his fingers in her face and wiggled his eyebrows.

She stared while he spoke, seeming to dissect every nuance of the odd language. He reached out, boldly wrapping his feeling arm around her neck, cleared his throat, and reverted to Castorian as he caressed her cheek with his right hand.

"My darling," he said softly, "we'll laugh, and by laughing, know a love greater than any other. Please tell me you feel the same way."

Seville's luscious lips formed into a smile. Her eyes sparkled with a disturbing, almost crazy gleam he had never noticed before. She raised her middle, sensitive hand.

"Pick two," she said. "Nyuk, nyuk."

THE END

The Circle Lady *
    By Bull Marquette
        *First featured on the radio program,
        Valley Writers Read on KVPR-FM, Valley
        Public Radio, on May 23, 2007.

Paul Conger's last summer before he started Kennick High came to a crashing end when his mother assigned him the awful task of baby-sitting his grandmother every night.

"She's lingering," his mother said. "Your Grandma's breast cancer has spread to her lungs. I'm sorry, sweetie, but here's a list of the things you have to do each evening. Afternoons, if she's stable, you can come home for a few hours."

She read the list aloud, but Paul's ears were ringing – of course he felt terrible for Grandma, but Mom might have been reading his own epitaph. The lazy sleepovers, cooking hotdogs over the campfire in the field, sneaking beers from Jasper's dad and drinking them on late night walks while they gazed up to pick out constellations in the sky – his whole vacation, gone in a sudden blitzkrieg. Gone, too, were their tantalizing debates about the Holly Park girls, and what a guy might do if one of those rich bitches ever said 'yes.'

"But, Mom." He interrupted her. "Jasper and Sam work, so night's the only time we have to strategize. How much longer do you think Grandma will live?" He bit his tongue, too late. "I didn't mean it like that."

Mom stared. "You watch your mouth when Death is in the house."

Paul fumed. "See? I love Grandma, but she's got you talking just like she talks," Paul said, and the alarm bells in his brain got louder. She was serious. "It's always visions, or omens about the weather, weird crap that makes me think weird. What if I slipped in astronomy class, and talked like she does? She doesn't understand science. Death is a result of disease, not some visit from a spook in a black hood with a grass cutter."

His mother took a long drag on her cigarette. "Maybe you don't remember when your grandfather died. Death came in, and wouldn't leave until it took Great Aunt Sally, too. And Mrs. Crenshaw."

Paul stomped his feet. "But Mrs. Crenshaw wasn't even our kin."

"Well, she lived next door," Mom said, and scribbled a new task onto her list. "Keep the trash can empty, or it will stink."

Paul remembered Grandpa's last moments all too well, remembered how a living, breathing creature with kind eyes and tobacco breath and rough whiskers and a gravelly laugh simply quit breathing. Forever. Paul dated his own incurable desire to explain things from that moment, but all that was beside the point. He was a growing boy on the verge of manhood, not a Medicare nurse. "I'll do it two nights a week. That's only fair. You and Aunt June can split the rest."

"She's already spitting blood." Mom said it quietly, completely ignoring his offer, and then she lit a new cigarette and slumped over in the posture she usually saved for when she was drunk and crying about how Dad's tour in the Middle East would never end. Paul's goose was cooked. "You know how nervous Aunt June gets, Paul. She's not up to dealing with it," she continued, but he was fighting back tears. "And if you want me to keep my job, I'll have to have some rest. You just clean up after her and put the rags in the wash. Come on, son. Some day, you'll be glad you did this for Gran."

He took one of her hands and fell to his knees. "Please. Not every night? The boys and I have to be ready for the fights."

"What fights?"

"The seniors at Kennick will zero in on any boy from North Central. That's why the three of us have to stick together."

"You get into a fight, I'll e-mail your father." She opened the icebox and began pulling out leftovers. "You know the cleaning's going to get worse, don't you?"

He rose, and stomped toward the doorway. Shaking now, he raised one fist, and delivered his final, quiet threat through clenched teeth. "Don't you dare start in about her bowels and stuff."

"I'm trying to prepare you. It's just for a while, Paul. Things will change when your dad comes home."

That night, Paul reported to his prison cell, the front bedroom of Grandma's house. She threw the windows wide open, letting the crickets sing through the screens like sirens, calling him out to run with the guys. Mom didn't even let him bring his I-Pod, because he was supposed to listen to Grandma, not his favorite MP3s. His only luxury was a tiny portable TV, with no sound, stuck on closed captioning, as if by design. But each time he thought about sneaking out for an hour or so, the old woman launched into a coughing attack that sent him cowering under the covers. How could life be this unfair to both of them?

"This is crazy," Grandma said after lunch the next day. "Tying down a growing boy like this. Tonight, when your mom says come over, you just say 'no.'"

"I don't mind," he lied. But the mile-long jog home felt like Logan's Run, and when he walked into his own kitchen and grabbed a soda from the icebox, the precious summer was his again for a few hours.

A routine developed. Each evening, Paul endured his mother's questions. Yes, some mornings the old woman just lay there, moaning. Yes, blood was coming more often. But he didn't dare reveal that on other days, Grandma sprang from bed like a girl, bossed him through his chores, then sent him home early so she could secretly walk down to North's Grocery to buy pork rinds. He knew her scheme, because one day he hid and followed her, and was waiting on the porch when she returned.

"Grandma, I'm going to tell," he threatened. "You know the doctors said you can't have those."

She hugged the grocery sack like a treasure, turned beet-red and flew into a coughing fit before she could fight back. When the retching stopped, she looked up at him, eyes fierce. "Go ahead, Boy, and just see if you get any more movie money." He took pity on her, and kept quiet.

One night during the third grueling week of his vigil, Paul lay on his pillows watching a silent Dave Letterman, when a shadow suddenly appeared in the hall. He jerked straight up and managed to switch on the lamp, illuminating Grandma in the doorway, just standing there in her slip, hair stringy, eyes wild, her lips framed by white moisture. "It's coming, Boy. You've got the Sight, just like me, so you oughta be able to see it," she said.

"Grandma, that's just superstition," Paul answered between gasps. She always wore her hairnet, and cared about her looks, so he had never seen her like this before. "The age of reason is here," he began, but her glare grew wilder, and he trailed off.

"Tell me you see it coming," she demanded.

Paul gripped the bed table, too winded to answer. After a long moment, she shook her head and turned back to her own room. But the damage was done. There was no mistaking that look. Grandma was afraid.

He curled up into a ball, and tried to forget that look. Perhaps he slept a little, for a loud knock at the front door woke him. Morning had come, and out on the porch, Sam and Jasper stood, hands in their pockets.

"Hey guys," Paul said. "Listen, if Grandma is feeling OK, let's meet at my house this afternoon."

"Sure. We don't have any lawns to cut today." Jasper smiled, then frowned. "Tell him," he urged Sam.

Sam took a deep breath. "Jasper and I are staying at Daley instead of going to Kennick."

"What? You assholes." Paul looked from one to the other. It was no joke. "Didn't your transfers go through?"

"It's not that." The two friends traded looks. "We'll make varsity at Daley a lot faster," Sam said. "Might even get girlfriends. Face it, Stud. At Kennick, guys like us don't stand a chance."

Paul gripped the screen door, wondering who decided to make this the summer from Hell. He exploded. "What about all your bragging, Jasper? Didn't we pledge to get a piece of those Holly Park girls? Where's your manhood?"

They both looked down. The porch floor needed a paint job. "Sorry," Jasper finally said. "Why ruin high school by trying to fit in with the snots?"

They stood for another shuffling moment, and then Sam said, "See ya," and they walked away.

That night, Paul turned off Grandma's light. "Night," he said.

"You gonna watch TV?" she asked. Her wheezing was louder, and she kept switching positions on the bed.

"I'll read a while. We're supposed to finish five books during the summer."

"This weekend is your last chance, Boy. What number you on?"

"Number four. But the last one's skinny."

"You're a good boy, Paul. I curse myself for never telling you that often enough."

"Thanks."

She coughed and cleared her throat. "I don't have to tell you what's happening. Don't ever forget you've got the Gift. You can *see* things others can't. Your mom don't show it much, but it skips a generation sometimes."

"Grandma, that's nice, but science teaches us there's no such thing."

"I'm glad you got good scores, Boy, but the Sight don't have nothin' to do with science," she insisted between hacks. "Remember the time you found the rat Yardley hid?"

"That rat was dead and stinking, Grandma."

"Well, it didn't die until your cousin got a hold of it." Her laughter brought on a new fit, but she flexed her fingers, a strange gesture, and he stayed. What if it happened tonight? He would be the only one here.

"Don't be obstinate," she said, serious again. "I'm talking about that other time, when it was still alive. He took it out of the cage and hid it under the leaves outside. Poor thing couldn't run off because it was ten degrees and sleet all over the ground. Remember?" It happened years ago. Paul remembered well, perhaps because it was the first pet they let him have, all for himself. "Your daddy was looking in the house, with Yardley playing like he was helping, but you marched out the back door and brought the poor little creature inside. The Sight led you to him."

"Yes, ma'am." It was too late to teach her that a good scientist, even a private eye, could have found the rat even more quickly than he did.

"I hate myself for saying it, but your cousin was a no-good, even when he was ten."

"Yardley's in Huntsville, Grandma. He can't bother anybody again for a long while."

He offered her a wet rag. She waved him away, but her voice followed him, soft, unnatural. "Them that has the Sight are called on to use it."

"What?"

"It's God's way."

"Yes, ma'am. Now try to sleep." He took the long way around, through the living room, seeking momentary relief from her rattling breath, but his own sad ghosts were waiting there for him. Over in that dark corner, he and cousin Mark used to play toy cars. The Christmas tree always occupied the front window. Grandpa's old exercise bike still sat beside the couch, even though it broke the day they discovered his cancer. A tear escaped onto his cheek without warning. What would they do with the house when she was gone?

Instead of reading, Paul turned off the light and counted all the ways a good detective might have tracked down Yardley's rat. You just had to study the delinquent's behavior to make a decent prediction. That's how the cops caught Yardley in the bait shop robbery. Maybe that was the saddest thing about Grandma's death, if and when it happened: she would leave this world without understanding the simple beauty of the scientific method.

The late August crickets sang until a coughing fit silenced them. Then another, and it seemed they would never start again. Jasper had said that with lung cancer, there would come a time when the coughing would start and never stop. Paul wondered how long to let it go on before he called the ambulance. He could call mom – but if it were a false alarm – A shiver started at his feet, and wouldn't stop until the darkness closed in on him.

A loud noise jolted him awake, and for a full, grinding minute it sounded as if she would never get her throat clear. Daylight pushed through the blinds, and the clock read thirty-six minutes after five. Soon he would be getting up early every morning to go to a school where he had no friends. He clenched his eyes shut and rolled over.

Then he heard the car. From the head of the bed, he could just see through the dusty living room, out the side windows to Foxwood Street, where a huge blue Cadillac was stopping at the curb.

Automatically, Paul pulled on his pants and shirt. An old woman struggled with something in the car's front seat. Odd, the way she was dressed up, hat and all. Then it dawned on him: she was some old biddy from Grandma's Church Circle. They came by every afternoon, these days, but five in the morning was ridiculous. Maybe she was some old farmwoman who thought the whole world rose at three.

"Is she here?" Grandma called out suddenly. Paul jumped.

"It's too early." He tried to shush her. "I'll get whatever she's bringing and send her away."

He went out through the front, and across the porch, kicking more childhood memories across the creaky floorboards. As if she expected curb service, the old biddy had not moved from the driver's seat. Her windows were automatic, and she rolled them all down, scowling. "Is Daisy awake?" she asked.

"Ma'am, it's early. Gosh--" Involuntary surprise. Close-up, her automobile was stunning, waxed and polished to a metallic blue perfection, with big taillights that fairly swooped up into the air. This was no farmwoman, but some grandma from one of Sironia's wealthiest families. "It's not a Caddy, is it? Mercedes?"

"Tell Daisy I'm here." An order, not a request, and Paul looked at her with new contempt. The wispy silvery veil that hung in front of her face, her velvet dress and a string of pearls that would choke a horse – she reeked of money.

He dared to lie. "She's asleep, ma'am. If you have a dish, I'll just take it in. But can I look inside your car?"

She regarded him without humor. "Go ahead. Stick your head in."

He leaned through the open window behind her, glancing around for whatever potluck she had brought, and punched at the plush, spongy seats. But the view out the rear window was all wrong – the houses and fences along Foxwood looked too far away. Paul reached to touch the glass, but it elongated, receding just as his fingers approached.

"What the hell?" he said. The window wavered, and kept stretching, all the way to Twentieth Street, then

Twenty-First, the glass twisting the morning sun into every color of the rainbow.

His stomach convulsed, and he recoiled, trying to jerk free, but his left hand stuck to the door handle like an icicle. He wanted to scream, but a glance at the vehicle's ceiling soothed his slamming heart. The headliner was dark, like the night sky, and even the stars were there.

"My God, what kinda car is this?" he cried. In the last week of junior high, he took a field trip to Kennick High's amazing planetarium. Here it was again – a dome of twinkling lights – but now each star was a double, twins. Not lights, but tiny holes through which tiny pictures seeped, scenes of daylight and darkness. He pulled closer, and peered into first one pair, then another, like looking into tiny microscopes. The scenes inside the dots of light were not just visual – they writhed with emotion, mostly anguish. A deep shiver traveled through his entire frame. He was perceiving the world through the eyes of hundreds, thousands of people facing the end of their lives.

"That's impossible," he yelled, thrashing and kicking, fighting to extricate himself from the window, but his fingers were still magnetized to the cold metal. The door wouldn't budge, and car's infinite interior swayed and wavered—

"Dizzy," he said, gasping, hoping the lady would have mercy, throw a switch to open the door or something. If he couldn't hold on, he would fall into the vehicle, and something told me those plush seats were *not* where he wanted to be. "Let me go," he cried.

A *Pop!* and he was free, falling back, rolling on the dew-soaked grass like someone with his shirt on fire, trying to put himself out. The Circle Lady climbed out of the car and loomed above him, and there was nowhere he could go, except to scoot backwards on his butt until he slammed against the cedar tree.

She draped her black purse over her arm. "Is Daisy coming?" Another demand. But Paul was falling down a well, hypnotized by the intensity of her eyes, as if a wind were blowing from them, freezing everything her gaze touched.

The sound of the back door shocked him awake. He scrambled to his feet. "I'll get her," he said. The Circle Lady took a step toward the gate, but Paul reached the latch first.

Grandma stepped out onto the back walk, clutching her own purse, dressed up for church. But this was Friday morning. "This way," he whispered, gripping her hand.

"Let go, Boy. I'm coming."

"No, Grandma. We have to go to North's."

"What?" She pushed through the gate with surprising momentum, and it was all Paul could do to force her off course. The Circle Lady waited patiently in the grass.

"North's," he said. "To get your pork rinds."

Grandma softened for an instant, and he seized that chance to push, angling her between the porch and the terrifying woman. With each rise and fall of Grandma's high-button shoes, Paul felt his muscles fluttering, weakening. He glanced over his right shoulder, his lungs crying for air. The Circle Lady extended her hand.

"I can't eat those," Grandma said suddenly. "I just remembered, they won't let me."

"Who cares?" Paul screamed, straining against the lead monolith his grandmother had become. "It won't kill you to buy one more bag."

Another glance – the terrifying woman's fingers floated gracefully, determined to touch Grandma, seeking an opening under Paul's arm, or over his shoulder. He dodged, careful to push his body between the two old women.

"I can't go any farther," Grandma whispered, her voice a fragile remnant of the past, as if the very presence of that infernal church woman could jam sound, the same way her dark eyes blotted out light.

"Move to the crosswalk." His own voice sounded muffled, too, and dry, like feathers rubbing together inside a pillow. Grandma took a step, but the Circle Lady's bulky shadow fell across their path. It was over, Paul realized. He had thought the woman was here just for Grandma, but now he understood his time was also up. His knees sagged, until he was bent over, and with his last ounce of strength, he looked up into Daisy Timmerman's eyes. "Please try, Grandma," he begged. "I love you."

Her gaze met his. Her eyes held tiny fires, like the ones in the car's ceiling, but these twinkles were still warm. She smiled, and when her shoes clomped down off the curb, onto the cement of the street, a peal of thunder rolled through the sky. As if a dam had broken, oxygen flooded into Paul's lungs, and he glanced over his shoulder. The Circle Lady was climbing back into her car.

He kept his arm intertwined with Grandma's for three blocks, all the way to North's. Incredibly, the store had opened early, and he led her to the aisle with potato chips and pork rinds.

"What were you thinking, Paul?" A stab of sunlight blinded him, and he sat up. His mother stood in the doorway, holding an unopened bag of rinds. Beyond her, he could see Aunt June fretting with several strange men dressed in white and khaki. Their huddle broke to let a bed on rollers through. Grandma lay on it, eyes closed.

He jumped up, but Mom shook the bag right in his face. "Three of these. In the pantry," she said, voice trembling. "Don't you know she has fluid around her heart?" He pushed past her just in time to see them loading Grandma into the ambulance.

Sunlight splashed the greens and blues of the last afternoon of summer through the windows of the hospital waiting room. Kids rode bikes on the street, laughing by, but Paul was here, stuck in yet another prison. His butt was sore, no matter how he shifted in the chair, and Aunt June jabbered to his mother incessantly, under her breath, determined not to let Paul hear any of her secrets.

He knew they would swing open the emergency room doors soon. Dr. Billings would come out, looking sad. But Paul didn't dare close his eyes, because every time he did, he saw the imprint of the Circle Lady's massive body inside his lids. He felt guilty for not telling Mom about her, even if it was only a dream. If Death was in the house, she should be alerted.

He rose and paced, steering clear of those bleary, waiting patients who coughed or sniffled. If only Grandma would come tottering out and convince the women to let him go, to spend this last raw afternoon with the boys. What the hell, he didn't want to go to Kennick, either.

Time dragged, until the door to the street opened, and a pretty blonde in a starched pink shirt came in and settled down with a family that had been waiting in the corner since before Paul arrived. She had brown hair, perfect breasts and a gold necklace she toyed with between her fingers while she talked. She avoided his gaze for more than an hour. Finally, he walked to the water fountain for the thousandth time, and when he turned, she was standing right behind him.

"Hi," he said. Instead of ignoring him, she smiled.

"I saw you over there," she said. "Who are you here for?"

"My grandmother had a spell. Too much salt. I kind of let her eat something she wasn't supposed to." He shut his mouth before he said anything else stupid.

"You let her?" Her brow wrinkled.

He shrugged. "Pork rinds. Her favorite, besides pretzels."

Fingers played along her necklace again, drawing his gaze to her shirt's pink fabric, and the way it laid against her perfect, suntanned neck. Someone called a name – Tracy – but before she turned away, she boldly leaned over and touched his arm. "I think she should be able to eat what she wants," she whispered.

The doors swung open and Tracy's family was summoned, and she turned and smiled before she disappeared with them. Paul shuffled back to find his ratty chair had turned into a cloud floating above the cares of the world, even beyond Aunt June's prattling. When he finally looked up, he saw that the waiting room clock read five-thirty-six, twelve hours exactly since the Circle Lady came. "She's going to be all right," he said automatically. The women just stared.

The next morning, he held the door of their Ford station wagon while a big male orderly helped Grandma into the back seat for the ride home. She raised a hand, and pulled Paul's head down close to hers. "You did good, Boy," she whispered. "But you don't have to do that next time. Granny's not afraid anymore."

During those first days at Kennick High, Paul barely spoke to anyone. In the halls, some strangers even introduced themselves, but when he looked at them, their faces seemed to morph, and cold wind came from their eyes. There was no one here who would understand. Hell, even if the guys were here, he didn't think he would tell.

Then, on the afternoon of the third day, he rounded a corner and merged with a wave of bodies crowding toward the stairs. She was there, holding the railing and chattering with her girlfriends. He froze. It was Tracy, the girl in the pink shirt. Today, she wore plaid.

Paul fell back against a locker and watched her climb those stairs. Deep inside, something relaxed. He wasn't afraid anymore, either.

THE END

The Nine Days of Barbara
By Bull Marquette

Day 1

The Christmas party fell on the night of the seven-month anniversary of Trent Davis' divorce. He felt ridiculous, driving through a sleet storm just to get drunk with a bunch of society snobs and put himself on display for old biddies who would look down their noses at the guy who moved from Cowan Estates to an apartment, but the infernal badgering of his few remaining friends finally won out. Or perhaps it was the tiny whisper of hope the Christmas season forced on everyone.

Cindy had taken his property and blackened his name as much as possible, even though she was the one who had strayed into the bed of another. His arc through the dizzying heights of Sironia's social set lasted not a day longer than their marriage. The party invitations went astray, no country club lunches, and the rich ranchers who used to collar him at Dolly's to suggest he run for school board no longer volunteered to buy his coffee. Even his sexual fantasies were ruined – how could one imagine pleasure in dreams where the heroine stabbed him in the back before he could even get excited. He sucked all that in and drove slowly through the ticking ice pellets, telling himself that Trent the Gladiator was once and for all back on the prowl.

The McCrackens' palatial home welcomed him with art deco warmth and pungent scents of pine and cinnamon and rum. On ice-covered roads, Sironians drove like schizophrenics. But even mortal danger can't keep rich people away from free booze, Trent thought as he sank into a five thousand dollar sofa. He endured Wheat-Thins and small talk about local politics while, out of the corner of his eye, he counted even more furtive, wry glances than he had expected. The cesspool Cindy had stirred up was still at high tide, and the few eligible ladies present couldn't swim. Besides, the room was too hot. He clacked his third eggnog onto the crystal coffee table and silently rehearsed his excuse to leave early. Then Barbara Benedetto squeezed his shoulder.

"Your drink is empty," she said, and moved toward the serving board. He had seen her at other gatherings over the years, but now she stood out, svelte in a black dress and pearls, with lanky arms and legs that posed like a dancer as she reached over bowls of goodies for the pitcher. Her maiden name was Smith or Jones, he seemed to remember, but she had married Primo Benedetto, the meat packer.

Barbara bent over to pour, and displayed her perfect cleavage right in his face, like a Christmas present he never asked for. By the time she straightened up, he realized he wanted the whole package.

Someone in the ballroom sat down at the piano and a round of soused carols began. Forms shifted, lights blinked, and Trent sucked the thick liquid, watching Barbara float easily among the centers of influence. Perhaps she knew she was being studied, because when he raised his empty, nog-coated glass, she attended again, filled it, then crouched down next to him, exposing one knee and part of her thigh. A smooth, tan highway to a Christmas wonderland.

"I hope you're not driving," she said with a giggle.

The laughter in the ballroom grew louder, the phrasing of *Wenceslaus* raucous, and his fifth drink unearthed courage Trent had left behind in college. He rose, and found her in a corner nibbling crackers with caviar.

"What do you do?" he asked, starting safely.

"I teach art history out at Sironia State."

"Whoa. You mean the old masters? Van Gogh, Rembrandt and Picasso? That sort of thing?"

Her smile broadened. "Very good. You know something about art?"

"You just heard my whole catalogue."

She laughed, enough to be generous. "Well, I'm just part-time. And I'm lucky to get that. Prim doesn't think a wife should work."

Trent's brain stopped for a moment, combing through data banks he had shut down on his wedding day. She kept mentioning her husband. Did that mean she was really married, or was it a cry for help?

"You going anywhere for Christmas?" he heard himself ask, straining not to slur, praying for guidance as to what he might say next. Cindy laughed him out of the room every time he laid a line on her. He splayed a hand on the wall for balance.

"Nah." Barbara shook her head and studied a new cracker wistfully. "Oh, Prim's going on his annual fishing trip at the end of the year."

"Really?"

"Yeah. They go to Cabo, and get a boat, looking for marlin. I guess the fishing's pretty good in years with El Nino."

"You mean he leaves you alone for New Years?" The window might be opening, but he was too rusty to be certain, and standing too close to her. Even so, the damnable Universe was trying to help, for once. The others had fled to the piano, leaving Barbara alone with him, and her magnolia perfume had its hooks out, pricking his doubts as quickly as they rose up.

"Afraid so," she said. "For a whole week. He leaves the night of the Twenty-Seventh, so I have to entertain myself until next year." Raised eyebrows and a laugh while fingers delicately rode the bumps of pearls. She put down her half-cracker, lifted a flute of champagne and whispered a toast. "To you."

Trent smiled and gave a mock bow, playing the part of someone with class. But his thymus gland was spewing lava.

"So --" He sighed, measuring an impossible, doomed invitation. The pause began grinding, and he imagined the piano crashing, sounding the alarm, bringing the revelers flooding in to surround him and catch him in mid-pass. He pictured Barbara running to Benedetto, himself, relaying the horrible suggestion now at its base camp in Trent's throat.

Stereotypical rumors of Mafia connections were wasted on Primo Benedetto. He was short and stocky, but wiry just the same, with a bald head shaped like a falcon, gestures too fast for his build, eyes too sharp to let much get past him. A man like him didn't need the mob for backup.

Even so, some things in nature can't be stopped. *God rest ye merry*, the carolers advised over the piano. Trent slurped eggnog and stared out the ice-crusted window. "So if I'm going to call you, it should be on the morning of the Twenty-Eighth?"

The lady looked away immediately, counting her pearls, and maybe her own heartbeat. Trent's pulse, by contrast, had ceased. His toes were off the cliff, and only God knew what lay below.

"That'd be OK," she said quietly. "But we can't meet at my house. Neighbors." A blush. And a smile.

"I live in an apartment since my divorce--"

Barbara shook her head. "We can't meet there, either. This big city is a little town."

The piano jangled to a climax, and the prissed-up elite swarmed back into the room, seeking refills. Another smile. "I have to help Janelle," Barbara said, and turned away. He watched the back of her legs as she walked. They were perfect.

Trent reached the coffee pot at the same instant that Mayor Gibson did. They argued the zoo-bond issue for thirty minutes, but Trent was careful to part on good terms.

"Such a lovely party," he told Janelle McCracken as he punched into his overcoat.

"Thank you, dear," she said. "So sorry about you and Cindy. Now be careful out on those streets."

The survivors were singing *Silent Night* when Trent paused in the doorway and looked back. Barbara was peering at him from a covey of elegant dresses and string-down coiffures. She smiled, and Trent rode Santa's sleigh all the way home.

Day 2

It was the worst Christmas of his life. For the first time, he understood why depressed people couldn't get out of bed. On nights when sleep did come, Barbara invaded his dreams. Invariably, she began to disrobe, almost reaching the magic point before Cindy burst in, pleading for forgiveness, cursing him for infidelity and threatening new lawsuits, all at the same time. Occasionally, there was a knock at his dream door, and Trent would open it to find Primo Benedetto glowering, holding his fish-cleaning knife. Each time he raised the dagger, Trent's alarm clock went off, and he would lie there in a cold sweat, wondering if Cindy felt this way when she was betraying him.

He scanned cases and wrote briefs with a vengeance on the twenty-seventh. Through his office's open window blinds, the weak winter sun glinted off of a passing airplane in the deep blue. The mid-morning flight to Dallas. Trent wondered if it carried Benedetto and his fishing goodfellows, bound for warm waters, booze and brotherhood. That's what he was plotting to betray, wasn't it? The very brotherhood of men. Turning the cuckold trick on a poor innocent man, the same way Rick Trautschold had done to him, assuming Rick was the only one that Cindy had crawled into bed with.

That night, his conscience nagged him more relentlessly than Cindy ever did, until he made the right decision: this was wrong. Wrong to waste Barbara's time, and his. Wrong to become the very sort of monster that he loathed.

Even so, the next morning he decided to keep his options open, like any good lawyer. "You can't take the afternoon off," Darla said, and huffed herself up to her full, squarish height. "The partners are on vacation, and Marilyn has a deposition in Houston."

"Who said I was taking it off?" he protested, hoping that this was the extent of Darla's mind-reading. "But I do have to make some calls. If a client summons me, oh, well."

He closed his door and mentally polished his withdrawal speech, keeping it light, funny, even while his hand hung over the phone like a vulture. Finally, he dialed her unlisted number – the one he found on the Internet after an hour of searching, and at a cost of fourteen-ninety-five.

Five rings. "Yes?" Her voice shook him to his marrow.

"Hi. It's me, Trent," he said, and was immediately out of ammo. "Trent Davis."

"Hi," she replied, softly familiar. "I was wondering if you would call."

"How about Hillsboro?" he said. "I mean, is your husband still on his trip?"

"Where in Hillsboro?"

"The Lucky Nine Suites. On the highway, across from the Outlet Mall." Saying the motel's name aloud made it sound even more tawdry. She was used to the Ritz, the Hyatt, the frigging Four Seasons. And in that instant he remembered his well-rehearsed speech of sane reasons that they should both shine this on. Was it too late to bring those up now?

"When? What room?"

"Give me your cell phone number, and I'll tell you when I get there. Three – no, two o'clock." His voice shook, and he knew she heard.

The desk clerk gave him a room overlooking the holiday traffic on I-35. Out across the rolling landscape, beyond the whine of Mac trucks, the Outlet Mall stores shone brightly against the gray clouds. A light sleet was falling again, as if an ice storm were mandatory each time he met her. That meant this couldn't last until summer, and the thought gave him some relief.

He stayed at the window, imagining hired enforcers in every car that skidded and slid into the crowded parking lot. P-I's hired by Primo himself, packing heat. He leaned back in the suite's single chair, stomach grinding, and wished she wouldn't come.

But a Mercedes finally dodged the off-ramp construction and pulled into the only empty slot in sight. She held up a purse to block the sleet, hiding her face, but the slender body was unmistakable, even draped in a long coat. The perfect legs protruded from beneath it, walking gingerly through the icy pellets. Then up the stairs, and Trent reminded his heart to begin pumping again. Should he kiss her when she came through the door?

"Hi," she said, smiling, and tossed her purse onto the chair. "Want to go shopping? They're having some great sales across the highway."

She might have used a baseball bat. He stuttered. "What do you want to buy?"

"Prim gave me a bum food processor for Christmas," she said. "I want the next model up." Thankfully, she let him take her coat, as if they really weren't going anywhere. She wore a striped wool sweater that fit her just right.

Sleet clicked against the window, and he clumsily drew the curtain. What now? Small talk? She had mentioned her husband again, and his gaze lit on the bottle of champagne that wouldn't fit into the honor bar fridge. Should he open it?

"Restroom," she said, raising a finger and disappearing into the bedroom, which he had stupidly left dark. He stood paralyzed, stomach acid churning. This was all so awful. He panted, and groped until he had the foil off the cork, and then he realized – he had forgotten to bring champagne glasses. That did it. He would offer her a plastic hotel cup, and she would see the sort of peasant she was dealing with. Then he could apologize, and they could go their separate ways out in the icy world.

"Don't open that yet." A soft voice stopped his fingers in mid-twist.

Trent turned. She was standing there, naked in the doorway. She held out a hand. "The champagne is for after," she said. He let her pull him into the darkness.

Day 3

It was Trent's fault for not suggesting future plans. He called her cell phone every night, but she didn't answer. If all she wanted was a one-night stand, she could at least pay him the courtesy of a goodbye.

On the afternoon of New Year's Eve, Trent bought two bottles of Bollinger and some brie. He phoned regrets to two different parties to which he'd been invited. At four o'clock, he dialed again, wondering if this were the way suicides felt when they popped the first pills into their mouths. It was a crime for her to greet the New Year alone in that huge house. Here, on his couch, making love by candlelight was the way a new era should be begun.

This time, instead of voicemail, he heard her clear her throat and begin speaking in a whisper. "He's back," she said. "Flew back early. Those guys he goes with always piss him off."

"But it's New Year's Eve," he said. "Any chance you can get away?"

"Of course not. Don't phone me. I'll call you in a couple of days."

She was barely audible, and he was yelling. "So what does that mean? January First? The Second? Barbara, I have to see you."

"Gotta go," she said. "Happy New Year." She hung up, and he pictured the jerk entering the room at that very instant. Maybe he would grab the phone away when it rang. Trent dialed again, anyway. Straight to message. But a different voice drowned out her perky recitation. The voice in his head. *This girl is trouble,* it said. *Let her go.*

On Monday morning, Basil Rook intercepted him at the office's back entrance, eyes wide. "Why didn't you tell us? He's been waiting fifteen minutes." Bony fingers snatched at Trent's overcoat.

"What? Who?"

"Primo Benedetto, of course. You idiot, you can't keep *him* waiting. Why didn't you tell him to talk to Roger or me if you were going to be late?" Now he had the coat, pushing from the rear, but Trent's stomach convulsed, and he managed to hook one foot around the door sill.

"No. I can't see him. What does he want?"

"Want? You ass, he's having trouble with Jenkins and Taylor. Go to the weekly lunches. How can you land clients if you don't stay up on the gossip?" Rook shoved him bodily into his chair and began collecting files from the desk. "It's his Four Hundred Acres development. General Motors has their eye on it. My God, man, it'll be the biggest deal ever to hit Sironia."

Trent leapt from the seat and grabbed the old man's arm. "He's not here on a legal matter."

"Of course he is. The powerful don't answer cold calls, they make cold calls. Some yahoo at the club must have given you a good reference."

"I don't belong to the club anymore."

"Why not? The golf course is where the deals are."

"Basil, send him away. I'm not kidding." But Rook was already opening the door. Trent grabbed his chair to keep from passing out, and imagined bullets ripping through its shiny leather finish on their way into his own body.

"Mr. Benedetto, please. This way," Rook said. The scrawny man with no hair and a hawk face wore a bulky ski sweater – Christmas gift from her? – Basil was speaking, too loudly, pressing Trent's hand into the wiry claw that hung beneath the sharp, dark eyes. Trent felt himself enveloped by the smile of the grim reaper. "Here's Mr. Davis," Basil said. "I'm afraid he was burning the midnight oil on a case. He's not usually late."

Primo Benedetto put his hands in his pockets, and Trent flinched, looking for the bulge of a gun. But they were too baggy. "Not a problem," Benedetto said, and sat down while Rook blabbered about a board meeting at the Randolph Country Club. Trent sank into the cold leather of the chair that used to be his safe haven, and focused mightily on containing his bowels.

"So," Trent managed to utter when Rook finally closed the door behind him. "How may I help you, Mr. Benedetto?"

The hawk bent forward. This time, a smirk. "Mr. Davis, do you believe in God?"

The jig was up. Any hope that the meat-packer might truly be here by some accident of fate died in the shuddering creak of Trent's chair. Death was a scrawny, Jersey-accented hawk of a bastard.

"No," Trent said. "I mean, yes."

"So do I." The Hawk reached into his pocket again, but and when the hand came out, it held only a card. "I found this in the cuff of my pants this morning. On my mother's grave, it was just sticking up there, a message out of the blue. A sign from God." He flipped it across the desk – Trent's *Rook and Peale* business card. "What the hell's that on the back? Your cell phone number?" he asked.

No, Trent had never given Barbara his business card, would never have been that clumsy, would have certainly done something more romantic, but here it was, and when he saw his own handwriting on the back, he remembered scribbling the numbers with the hotel pen while this man's naked wife stuck her tongue in his ear. Her tongue – for an instant, the memory glistened like a star on the horizon. He took a deep breath.

"Are you having some legal difficulty, Mr. Benedetto?"

"Damn straight." The Hawk craned himself over the desk and reclaimed the card. "Confidential, right?"

Trent nodded.

"I especially don't want you to whisper a word to Smilin' Jack out there." He looked away, following his own gesture, and when the beaked head swiveled back, his eyes were brimming with tears. Trent was caught off guard. "They said you're a pretty good divorce guy. I think my wife is running around on me."

He paused, and stared. Fishing, Trent thought. He knew, but didn't know *who*. But was Trent on the list of suspects?

"I got family back in Chicago," Benedetto continued. "People depend on me, so I gotta be sure. If I'm gonna claim adultery, it's gotta stick. Otherwise she gets the whole wad. Ain't that how the courts work down here in Texas?"

A ham hand rubbed the wet eyes. They held a strange glint. The man was diabolical. Trent shuddered, and started chewing on his finger without meaning to. "This isn't about the Four Hundred Acres that GM wants?" he asked.

The Hawk recoiled. "Hell, no. I need someone to confirm that my wife is screwing around."

Sensing a way out, Trent avoided his gaze and began scribbling furiously. "That's a job for an investigator, Mr. Benedetto. Here's an agency I can refer you to."

A hand reached over and stopped the pen. "I don't want no private dick. One of those creeps photographs her in the act, it's on the Internet next morning." He let go. "You work the big divorces for the crazies around town, right? Maybe you know my wife? I'm sure I've seen you around at some of the dinners."

So it was just an act. A sick charade. The man *knew*. Trent wished he kept a pistol in his desk. "I know who she is."

"Then you understand why this can't get out. Even my best friend would be on her like a tick on a hound if they thought she was sleeping around." Hands raised, palms-up. "God's punishment for marrying beauty."

Trent sagged deeper into the chair, wondering if it wouldn't be better just to plead guilty. He was the transgressor, and the insanity defense was always admissible in cases with a woman like Barbara. He steeled himself. "Mr. Benedetto, I think we both know what's going on. So let's dispense with any more play-acting."

Maddeningly, the hawk wasn't paying attention, but absorbed by Trent's business card again, flicking it back and forth. Had he even heard? "Mr. Benedetto," Trent insisted. "What is it you want from me?"

The hawk kissed the card like a rosary, and stood up. "Let me take you to lunch," he said.

Trent braced. "I can't."

"Bullshit. If you're going to help me, you have to meet the wife up close. You got a fresh perspective, Davis. They tell me you've been through this, yourself. Divorce, I mean. I just want you to meet her, shake her hand, watch her eyes. Like when you nail some murderer on the witness stand. Then, when she's out of the room, you can tell me if she's two-timing me."

"No." Trent tightened his grip on the chair. He was too good. Was there still a chance he didn't know? "I'm not a private eye and I'm definitely not a mind reader."

"Davis, if I'm going to hire you--"

But Trent yelled, drowning him out. "Damn it, if you suspect her, just ask her. If she's running around, there's gotta be a reason--" he started, but stopped before it all came out.

The man looked thunderstruck. He sat for a moment, lips pressed together, and slowly answered with the only weapon Trent didn't know how to combat: silence. The beady eyes puddled-up again, and a hand rose to cover them.

Trent fidgeted, lost his grip, and stood up, shaking, hearing his own voice say the suicidal words. "I've got a court appearance this afternoon. Can I take my own car?"

Primo Benedetto's architectural masterpiece was one of a handful of mansions that all socialites in Sironia coveted. Cindy had always prayed for an invitation to this mausoleum, but cattlemen and anyone else connected to a meat-packer were, ironically, beneath her orbit. The entry was a half-moon, open-air salon that led to big double doors. Trent was struck by the ostentation more than he wanted to be, and let his guard down long enough to imagine himself sitting at that broad dining table, gazing at Barbara by candlelight, her divorce over and she with the deed to the house.

"Let's eat in my office, so she'll think it's all business." His walk was as sure and forceful as any of his gestures. He led Trent into a cozy den of built-in bookcases and glass display boxes full of rare coins. "Barb, guest for lunch. We need sandwiches." He called it out at the top of his lungs, the way one might alert a maid.

Hearing the man call her by a nickname was a painful glimpse into their intimacy, and for a moment,

Trent's guilt yawned before him like a chasm. The guy had set the stage beautifully: He could shoot them both in this room, and when his lawyer tracked Trent's Visa card to the Lucky Nine Suites' booking computer, any jury in Texas would acquit the wronged husband.

Trent lowered himself into the offered chair, but came back up just as quickly when the Red Sea parted, bolts of lightning flew and Barbara Benedetto came in from her kitchen. Her silky black blouse was covered by a bright blue apron that barely concealed her short skirt. Her eyes flared when she saw Trent. "Yes?" she asked, too innocently.

"You've met Mr. Davis, haven't you, hon?" the tycoon said. "He's a lawyer. I'm hiring a new bunch of vultures to ride herd on the first bunch."

His laughter filled the room, and her hand came forward, and the warmth of her grip set the continents back onto their rickety plates. "Nice to see you again, Mrs. Benedetto," Trent said, wondering if his performance were necessary, or if they were both just Primo's fools.

A weak smile, and she looked away. "Charmed. What did you want, Prim?"

"BLTs," he said, then looked at Trent. "You eat meat, right? Two BLT's on wheat, Doll. Pronto."

Then she was gone, and Trent was alone in an empty courtroom, waiting for both verdict and sentence. But that was a doomed strategy. The look in Barbara's eyes – was it fear or panic? He had invaded her domain – but through no design of his own. He touched the ornate desk, reaching for anything solid, and decided to try to talk things down to a civilized level. "Mr. Benedetto, why don't we both level with each other? Like in the old days, there's no reason why two gentlemen--"

Benedetto turned on him, as if surprised to find him there. "Get any vibes from her, yet? Nah, that was too fast. When she brings the food, I'll try to get her talking so you can look for clues."

"Come on." Trent slapped the desk. "You know that's not the real reason I'm here." The damned snake just wouldn't come out of his hole, but Trent was resolved not to admit anything until he was actually accused.

The phone rang, and Trent jumped a mile. Benedetto lifted the receiver, and his dark eyes faded for a vast minute. "What?" he finally cried out, forcing another flinch. "Tell him we've been waiting six weeks already." Cheeks turned red. "I don't give a damn--" Fuming, the scrawny man rose, waving for Trent to stay put. "Excuse me for one minute." Primo clomped across the polished ochre tile, past the Southwestern couches, through the French doors and out onto the patio that flanked the Olympic pool. When Trent looked around, Barbara entered, carrying a tray with two iced-teas on it.

She set it down, slowly, perfectly, as if allowing time for her perfume to bait the hook. She knelt, a replay of her movements at the McCrackens' party, and looked directly into Trent's eyes. "I've never been so turned-on in my life," she said.

Her hands intertwined with his. "No," he said. "Not here." But she pulled him from the chair, out of the patio's view, and he foolishly permitted a long, wet kiss.

"He'll be forever," Barbara whispered. "I can't stand it." She pulled, walking him behind Primo's plush chair, and touched a button on the desk. With a barely audible *click*, the bookcase sprang away from the wall, exposing a dark room. The pungent scent of tobacco stung his nostrils. She pulled at the movable wall, letting in more light, exposing racks of dusty wine bottles. It was a gigantic humidor, too – he could see boxes of cigars set neatly on shelves. At their base, several ancient-looking frames were stacked sideways. Paintings – the one facing him, a horse in oil.

"Is that your collection?" Trent whispered, his ears acutely tuned to Primo's muffled bellering out on the patio. She only tightened her grip, and maneuvered him through the opening, and into the cavern of cigars and wine. There was a metal handle on the back of the bookcase, and she pulled that, too, plunging them both into blackness. He fought half-heartedly, but she directed his hands, making them remember her silk blouse, the short skirt under her apron, and – no panties.

"Sweet Jesus, he'll find us," Trent said, and stumbled back. A single slit of light illuminated nothing, and surely Primo was finishing his call, coming back in, and Trent's foot crashed into the artwork, but her mouth was on his, and he breathed violently through his nose, sucking in nicotine air, laced with mold.

"Barbara, he's coming in," he gasped, certain he heard the far-away creak of the patio door, but she unzipped him and climbed, folding her arms around him, smothering him with her tongue. He had never done it standing up before, and his free hand flailed blindly against the wall for balance – he gripped a shelf, then wooden cigar boxes, caressed smooth glass bottles, always grasping, higher up the wall, until he pinched the fur, the cold glass eye and finally the prickly horns of some taxidermied beast.

Metal racks clanked, silk slipped between his lips, and her soft moans escaped into the darkness. With a last, mighty movement, she fell back, and a bottle crashed to the floor. "Leave it," she whispered, and then she was down, tiptoeing through a broader shaft of light. Trent expected hawk eyes to peer into the cave, but there was only a red lake around her bare feet. Wine or blood?

"Are you hurt?" he whispered. He brought out the monogrammed handkerchief he never used, and bent down, desperate to heal those perfectly tanned feet, even if it be his last act. She pushed the wall open wider. "Only a tiny cut," he reassured her, daubing the thin scratch.

Instead of thanking or kissing him, she tossed her hair like a defiant mistress in some French movie, stepped out onto the wide tiles, and waved him back to his place.

"You've got a smart mouth, you son-of-a-bitch--" Primo's voice, still beyond the French doors. She clicked the bookshelf wall back into place, then regarded Trent foggily.

He collapsed into the chair, his chest still heaving. "The wine will soak your picture frames," he said.

"I'll clean it up later. He's playing golf."

She turned, and escaped across the million dollar floor, leaving tell-tale footprints on the tiles. When she reached the deep-pile, multi-colored Oriental rug, her tracks disappeared, and he watched her long legs that began just below the apron until she vanished around a corner. This time, the patio door opened for real, and Trent reached shakily for a glass of tea. He created a smile, and locked his jaws together, forcefully swallowing the fluid that was gurgling up from his stomach.

"That was Marthedal," Benedetto said. "My foreman. He says I'm crazy to suspect her." Waiting, he planted two elbows.

Trent stammered, "I-I don't understand. You told your foreman?"

"What if he's right? What if I'm being too hard on her? I admit I'm paranoid." Benedetto's eyes drilled for another moment, then he fell back, and perused the ceiling's crown molding. "Billy Marthedal says all she needs is a baby, so why don't I get her one?"

He bent forward and began fidgeting with a clear plastic paperweight in which tiny, golden jet airplanes were suspended. "You might as well know. I'm firing blanks. No sperm count at all. My second wife made me get a vasectomy. Got it reversed, but it's all screwed up." He slapped the desk, and Trent held onto his glass. "I don't want to raise no stranger's kids. They at least gotta be hers. Does that make sense?"

Trent nodded, not sure what he was agreeing to.

"I've thought about this for a hundred years, but I keep coming back to the same thing, ya know?" Beseeching now, hands outstretched, like a hapless husband on the witness stand, but Trent was planning strategy more than listening. A jail break. If he stormed into the kitchen and asked her, would she run with him now, out of this place?

"So the kid has to be hers, which means artificial insemination, or whatever they do. But there's something horrible about that. I mean, what if there were a nice guy who could be the father but he would keep his nose out of my business and not ever be a threat, maybe never even see the kid?" He pointed. "You're the attorney. Can we do a contract like that?"

Trent's arms sagged. If she left the house without planning it, she might never get back in. He set his glass back onto the tray with two hands. Did the bastard miss the wine footprints on purpose? Half of Trent's being warned him to be very afraid, but the other half was slavering for her next entrance. "Maybe," he said.

"How about you?" The hawk eyes caught Trent's gaze and reeled it in.

"What?"

"You're a frigging lawyer, so you gotta have some intelligence in your genes. How 'bout a roll in the hay with the missus? Just once or twice. I'll pay you plenty. I like you, Davis. And remember, God pointed you out to me. Whaddya say?"

Trent gulped air, but it was devoid of oxygen. A layman might mistake the look in the monster's eyes for sincerity, but two hundred home-wrecking cases had taught Trent how to recognize evil. Besides, no one could be that *dumb*.

"You're cooler than any sicko I've ever represented," Trent said, and stood up. "I'm not your plaything. You may be under the delusion that she is, but I'm going to put a stop to that, too."

It was wrong to leave her here, alone with him, but he walked. If he fought the war now, he would lose. It had to be in the courtroom.

At eleven o'clock that night, the phone rang. "Hello?" Trent said dazedly.

"I can't believe what you did today." Her voice. "No one ever stood up to him like that."

"Barbara? Are you all right? You're not safe, because that guy is nuts. Let me come get you."

"I'm fine. He went to Del Monico's, so I'm alone. Thinking about you. Trent?"

"Yes?"

"I think I'm falling in love with you."

Day 4

He dialed her number several times each night, but the cell phone barrier had descended again, leaving her velvet voice to recite the same bright message repeatedly. For three days he analyzed her silence in every way possible. She didn't want him. Or she did, and didn't trust herself. Or she didn't really care, but theirs was a chemical reaction that couldn't be stopped when the two of them drew close together.

But Primo Benedetto was an ogre, the type Trent saw every month or so in his practice. Which reduced Barbara, a vivacious, sensuous creature, to the level of slave. Trent wasn't even sure he wanted it to continue, but did he lack the chivalry to at least try to free her?

After an unsatisfying TV dinner one night, he could stand the silence no longer, and he drove through the evening chill and parked his car in the driveway of a house for sale near theirs. He started climbing the fence, hoping to glimpse her through the wall of windows in the house's rear. But halfway up the neatly cemented stones, he noticed a trip-wire strung across the sharp metal points along the top. He gave up and went home.

The next morning, Trent took his *Mont Blanc* and checked through the appointments he would cancel. In the middle of the night, the better plan had come to him: he would drive by Benedetto's Meats, confirm that the bastard's car was there, then head out to the college. Barbara taught classes on Tuesday and Thursday mornings.

He looked down at the pad – her name, "Barbara," had been written a dozen times by the lazy pen. She had become an obsession. That had never happened before, and a voice inside shamed him. Obsessions broke up homes, emptied bank accounts, wrecked lives and usually wound up crashing in flames once the whiskey or drugs ran out, or clandestine meetings stopped being clandestine. Darla interrupted.

"Mr. Cantor will be thirty minutes late, and there is a Mrs. McCracken here to see you. She says it's private business, and she won't take long."

Like a fighter hit squarely in the stomach, Trent could only gesture. He retrieved his breath while Janelle found her seat. She wore the diamond necklace Casey McCracken bought her with winnings from his thoroughbreds. Overdressed for shopping.

"Good morning, Mrs. McCracken."

A tight smile. "Trent, I think you know why I'm here."

"I'm sure I don't." He knew it was a mistake the instant he said it. In Sironia, the lawyers outranked the politicians, and doctors were above lawyers. But the socialites held the top of the pyramid, and no one sat higher than this woman. It wasn't wise to lie to the Pope.

She ignored his gaffe, and began counting off points on her fingers. "Trent, Barbara Benedetto and I are taking flower arranging and origami classes together. She tells me everything. *Everything.* You're toying with the affections of a married woman, young man."

"I'm not toying." He hadn't expected to feel this naked.

"Calling her cell phone every night is toying, Trent. Didn't it occur to you that Primo could check her call log and see who's ringing at all hours?"

"She can put the ringer on mute." The lamest reply possible, he realized. He closed his eyes, letting the wave of humiliation wash over him, a feeling he knew well by now. He wondered in which tea room Janelle would be reporting this very conversation this afternoon.

"Is it the money?" she asked. "If there's a divorce, she won't get a lot of money. Primo's a smart cookie, and he's got a tough lawyer."

"I'm his lawyer," Trent heard himself mutter.

"Don't be ridiculous."

"Did she ask you to talk to me?"

"Not in so many words. But I care about her. And you, believe it or not. We all think you got the raw end when Cindy left you."

The royal *we*. Trent checked his watch. Her second class would end in fifteen minutes. If she didn't let the students go early, he might just make it. "For the record," he said. "I know you're concerned with Barbara's welfare, but she's a grown woman. If she wants me to disappear, she simply has to call me, or meet me somewhere and tell me to my face."

"That's not how it's done, Trent." She rose, brushing down the wrinkles on her dress. "Her husband's a bully. He checks everything she does, goes through the phone bills, even has her followed in broad daylight. But you – Barbara's worried. She told me Primo has a shotgun. If he catches you together, he'll use it."

Trent held on to his smile. "Please tell her what I said."

Before he could leave through the office's back door, Rook descended on him. "My friend, we need a report," he said. "Are you going to land the Four Hundred Acres account or not?"

"I may know more in an hour," Trent said, and stepped outside.

He drove, windows up against the crisp January air, silently calculating the billable hours this gamble was costing him. The stench that hung over Primo's slaughterhouse was suffocating, but had the effect of oil thrown on Trent's fire of excitement. The jerk's car sat in its reserved spot in front, and only minutes later, Trent guided his own car into Sironia State University's crowded maze of streets.

The art building was the oldest one on campus, and he parked next to it, against a red curb. The stairs creaked so loudly, Trent feared the wood would break under the weight of all the milling students. Between classes. Was he in time? A frosted-window on a door on the second floor bore Barbara's name, along with someone else's, both preceded by the title – "Prof." He opened it.

Her desk was closest to the door, and she looked up, arms laden with books, purse over her shoulder. "Oh, hi," she said, and her eyes lit up with everything but *goodbye*.

"Hi. I thought--" He stopped talking, and pushed the door full open. Her face clouded, part blush, part fear, maybe, and she glanced toward the far corner of the old-smelling office. Her office-mate's desk was stacked with papers, but the chair lay empty.

"This is risky," Barbara said, her cheeks fully crimson now, but she seemed too breathless to explain what "this" was.

"Thought we might have a hamburger," Trent said, reciting his script, though he knew that was impossible now. One hand gripped her elbow, while the other clicked the door to.

"Mindy will be back." Her books were a momentary obstacle, but she met his lips eagerly.

"When?"

Her volumes thudded to the creaky wooden floor while he pushed her against the desk, and up onto it. "The window's cold," she said, and he reached one hand around to cradle her against the ancient, warped glass. "No. Not here. This is impossible." But her kisses never relented, and she helped his other hand move rapidly beneath her dress. "Careful." The floor, the desk, the whole world creaked, and a herd of chattering students shuffled by, just outside the door.

They finished before it ever occurred to Trent that outside passersby could certainly see *something* through the steamed-up windows, if only they looked up to the second floor. While Barbara melted in his arms, he glanced out. College life, bright colors through the limbs of bare trees. Miraculously, her office mate still had not come through the door.

He kissed her ear. She stroked his hair, and climbed down to reassemble herself. He fell back, head resting on book spines in her stuffed shelves. "Janelle delivered your message," he said.

"I sent no message."

"But you spilled your guts to her."

She shrugged. "So? Everybody's entitled to a confidante. You're bound to have told somebody."

"Lawyers don't have confidantes. They're dangerous."

She had her underwear back on, and the books safely stacked on the desk, and scowled while she brushed her hair. "Janelle doesn't speak for me, Trent."

"Is it true you want me to quit calling?"

"Yeah. For now."

A pause. He died, and could not come back to life, even when she put the brush away.

"I'm sorry." She finally spoke again. "I'm too confused to let this keep happening."

"You can divorce him, Barbara. I don't care what he's told you. He can't get everything, not in this state.

You're a beautiful young woman. You have rights." He reached over and gripped her soft shoulder.

She looked down. Outside the door, the noisy crowd had died away.

"That was quite a performance he gave the other day," Trent said, not letting go. "He does know it's me who's calling, right?"

She shrugged. "He's going crazy. Two sons in their twenties, and now he wants to start another family."

"He told me."

Still gazing at the floor, she began dabbing her eyes before he even realized she was crying. "He promised we wouldn't have kids. That was one of my rules. A child makes it permanent, you know?"

"So it's not permanent? Is that because you knew he was a monster even before you married him?"

She bucked herself up, and threw him a disgusted sort of look. "I'm leaving him."

She rested on the desk again, and through the windows behind her, the winter wind had picked up, moving the oaks, making the old building whistle and groan. She was a painting, Trent thought, like the ones she must teach in her classes. Smooth skin, eyebrows perfect, lips exquisitely soft, and that was the tongue that coursed through his sideburns, setting off explosions only moments ago. Her tears stopped, and a majestic shudder passed through her. She was a little girl lost, and Trent the Gladiator was the only one who could lead her back to the life she deserved.

"Barbara, I'm pretty good with these types of cases. Come to my office tomorrow, and we'll sit down and make a list of the times he's abused you. Did he ever hit you? Or force sex?"

"You mean like what you just did?"

"Stop it. Did he ever humiliate you in front of your friends? Hiring private detectives to follow you can be a form of mental cruelty, and that we can document."

"I don't want his house. I just want enough money to start a new life," she said quietly.

"And I want to be part of that new life." He took her shoulders again, and she let him. "I've never been this hot for anyone. But we have to talk, get to know each other better. With me, you could teach full time. Or we could have a family – but you said you don't want one. Never mind. We'll do what's right for both of us, not push each other into more mistakes."

It was the proper speech to make to the next woman he married. Promises, bold and sweeping, and here he was making them years before he ever dreamed he would. Should he be at this point already? Was she the one? Winter threatened outside, while her office had grown insufferably hot. She met his eyes with a look he had no chance of deciphering.

"You're not listening, Trent. I'm leaving him tonight. He'll get some legal eagle from New York who'll pay off the judges. That means I'll be broke again. That's what I'm facing. Will you really want me when I'm destitute?"

"You won't be. Even with my payments to Cindy, I'll make enough money for us to get by."

She turned, and collected her books, and he might have left the room, for she was speaking more to herself than him. "How did you pass the bar exam? The correct answer is, no, you won't want me if I'm poor. Or you'll think you own me, like he does."

"Barbara."

She moved too quickly, and had the door open before he could react, and a bookish woman outside seemed startled, and moved out of her way.

"Barbara," Trent repeated, but dared nothing else in front of the newcomer, who just smiled at him as she crossed the threshold. Barbara was gone in a creak of stairs. When he got down to his car, he called her cell number. Her bright voicemail voice answered.

Day 5

Soon after he arrived the next day, Darla entered Trent's office with a deposition transcript. Rook crowded in behind her, wagging his finger in the air. "Look, Old Boy, Four Hundred Acres is on the front burner. Coltharp says GM may be looking downriver, too. You're going to have to let the old dinosaurs lend a guiding hand. We want to see your proposal today."

Trent gritted his teeth. There would be no proposals until he knew what happened to Barbara last night.

"Who?" Darla spoke loudly, something she never did in front of the partners. "I'm sorry, Mr. Rook, about whom were you speaking?"

"General Motors, my dear." He raised his eyebrows, looking smug. "And Primo Benedetto."

"Oh, didn't you hear?" She posed, licked her lips, and gave forth like a schoolgirl with a mouthful of gossip. "Mr. Weems was here. He said Benedetto Meats closed its doors this morning. The old man handed out severance checks at the gate. He's moving to Denver."

Trent stopped writing. Perhaps his jaw dropped, but he was sure his own expression was nothing like the look of horror pasted on Rook's countenance. "What happened? Is his marriage breaking up?" Trent heard himself say.

Rook stepped between them, blocking Darla from view. "Denver? Are you sure? Denver?" Then he swiveled, and banged the desk. "What the hell did you do to him, Davis?"

Trent mumbled some excuse, but his words didn't matter. Only seconds passed, but when he looked around, both his paralegal and his boss had disappeared. He left through the back door and drove to the Benedetto Estate. A security guard stopped him at the mailbox at the start of the driveway.

"Sorry, no visitors," he said.

"I'm here to see Mrs. Benedetto," Trent demanded.

"Can't see anybody. Nobody to see."

Trent took his foot off the brake and let the car roll. "I'll just be a minute. She's expecting me--"

But a pudgy hand gripped a windshield wiper, as if that would hold the entire car. "Mister, these folks left for Dallas this morning. Tomorrow they drive to Denver. And if you go down to that house, I'm calling the cops."

The guard's look was all business. Trent shifted into reverse, then, in an afterthought, pushed the gearshift all the way into park. "Look," he said, facing the hostile jury of one, "it may come as no surprise that Mr. and Mrs. Benedetto were having some marital problems. In fact, I'm the lady's lawyer, and it's illegal for her to be held incommunicado against her will."

He kept his movements large, overacting to deter any answer. He pulled his wallet from his coat, opened it, and produced two one-hundred dollar bills. He tried to smile like Mitch Simmons, the most shyster-y lawyer he knew. "I'm sure you don't want to be named in any lawsuit if the lady actually gets hurt, do you?"

The guard didn't flinch, but turned rapidly and walked over to a dated pickup truck parked behind the front hedge. He returned with a small metal toolbox, opened it, and held the box below the bills. "In here," he said. Trent dropped them, and the lid clanked shut. No money had changed hands. "Hyatt Galleria," the guard said, and waddled back to his truck.

Trent entered Dallas just as the sun was setting. The scene back at the office had not been pretty, but he would mend fences with Rook tomorrow. Tonight would be a siege, but his goal was to return with his distressed damsel, take her into his bed, show her what normal life was like with someone who really loved her. Failing that, he had printed off a list of Dallas' women's shelters. If she simply demanded to be moved to some other top-shelf hotel, he wasn't sure how much credit was left on his Visa card.

He had settled on a strategy during the two-hour drive up – pay off a bellhop for the room number when Primo was sitting in the bar. Anything to just get her alone. The plan's flaw was that he had only a single hundred left.

First, he tried the house phone – bingo, the Benedettos were registered. It still didn't make believable that they were really here – or that a man would give up a million-dollar business just to keep his wife in chains. Primo answered, and Trent hung up. A sandy-haired young man with a book sat in a plush lobby chair, and seemed a little too interested in his actions. Trent chalked it up to jangled nerves.

He found a seat in the Mustang Bar, right in the window where he could watch the lobby, and waited. If they ordered room service rather than going out to dine, he would have to go to Plan B, and bribe the front desk girl for more information – problematic, because that would certainly require a trip to the ATM, and his bank account might not stand the pressure. Unfortunately, the sprawling hotel had three large restaurants, two of them on the ninth floor. After a few drinks, he started circulating between all three.

A little after seven, his head hurt and he felt like an automaton plodding between suspicious glances in the lobby, the elevator and restaurant foyers. He decided on one last circuit, growing more desperate each time he envisioned her alone with that ogre, watching TV helplessly from a hotel bed. Or worse. But when he nodded and smiled at the hostess in Livingstone's Bistro for the twentieth time, he looked past her shoulder and his heart began to race. There they were, seated in the far corner, overlooking the brightly lit shopping center.

Primo's hands were flying, apparently instructing the waiter on the art of opening wine, with Barbara looking forlorn, eyes downcast, not noticing Trent yet. The place was too expensive to be crowded, and Trent asked for table near the front, just in view. If she started glancing around, she would see him before the ogre did, and maybe she could make some excuse about going to the bathroom.

He sat, accepted a menu and flapped open his napkin. A tall shadow fell across the table. He looked up – the sandy-haired guy from the lobby smiled, and sat down. "Mr. Davis? How are you?" Trent's mind raced, trying to figure where he had met this character before, but there was no need. Sandy slapped a folded Dallas County court document down in the middle of Trent's place setting. "That's a restraining order, Mr. Davis. And I'm afraid you're already too close to Mrs. Benedetto for us to allow you to stay here."

"Oh?" Trent's heart pounded, and he didn't know whether to slug this creep, or save it for Primo. "I guess I can have dinner anywhere I like." From the corner of his eye, he thought he saw Barbara look over, and recoil.

"Make this easy, Davis. You don't want to lose your license."

Trent opened his mouth to speak, then shoved the table into Sandy's midsection. Utensils clanged and the flower vase crashed behind him, but he was moving, dodging white-clothed, immaculate tables. "Barbara, come with me," he called out over the heads of the scattered diners.

She raised her napkin, and buried her face in it. Primo turned full around, eyes wild, but two thick men exploded from a table on the side and had him by either shoulder before he could get close.

"Come on, Jackass," one said, and stepped on his foot.

The pain shot up Trent's leg, but he squirmed away. No good – the goons were quick, anticipating every move.

Trent lunged, and almost reached the table. "Barbara, get up." Her shoulders shook – she was sobbing. "He can't do this to you."

"Sure he can," the other man said, and they had him, rushing him through a klatch of leering waiters. The sandy-haired one waited at the door, smiling even bigger than before, and in the same instant that they slammed Trent against the back wall of the elevator, the process server leaned in, and shoved the court order into his coat, ripping the pocket as he did.

"He's a wife beater, you scum," Trent yelled.

"Shut up." The first goon dug his index finger into Trent's forehead, and all three crowded in around him. On the first floor, a broad-shouldered cop was waiting. He slowed things down, like good policemen do, speaking deliberately, ignoring Trent's protests that the two bodyguards had no right to hold his arms.

"I'll sue every one of you," Trent said sternly. "Your jobs – every one of you."

The cop snatched the court order and slapped his face with it. Trent was driving back down I-35 before his heart slowed down enough for him to think of other threats he should have used.

He reached home a little before midnight. A message flashed on the phone and he played it. "Mr.

Davis, we do not suffer attorneys who willfully break the law." Basil Rook's voice bellowed through the room. "Your services are no longer needed at Rook and Peale. You may collect your severance check Friday. Goodbye." Trent poured the last of his bourbon into a cocktail glass, turned off the lights and sat down at the kitchen table. Finding her in Denver was going to be infinitely harder.

Day 6

Why had he even met Barbara? To Trent, Fate was the only answer that made any sense – and that made no sense whatsoever to his logical mind. Fate was like an eternal, invisible nemesis that had moved him from city to city in childhood, tearing his parents apart, putting them back together again, never letting his life settle to anything bearable until that second semester in law school when the professors started praising his mock briefs – for what reason, he didn't know.

He married Cindy, and she delivered him into the Sironian nobility, and a lifestyle he had only heard about. Until Fate got up Cindy's dress – with no provocation from him – and turned the world topsy-turvy again, stripping away half his income and casting him back adrift.

Now the fickle demon had offered Barbara to him, like some sort of life raft, only to rip her away, and return her to the arms of that creep. Maybe Fate was only nasty in this mendacious little town. Sironia held no more allure for Trent, if Barbara lived elsewhere. Only a fool would stay and try to recapture the status of big fish in a little pond. He had to follow her.

That was when the elusive nemesis suddenly decided to smile again, in the guise of Morris Cameron, one of the lead lawyers of Johnson, Connally and King, the second largest law firm in Big D.

"Screw Denver," Cameron said, sloshing a Mai Tai and punching Trent in the arm. They sat together at the bar right after Toby Jeep's wedding, fast friends in the space of two hours. "You definitely don't want to study for another bar exam. Hell, just move to Dallas, get established, then truck on up to the mile-high city, talk turkey with the bitch and bring her home."

Trent nodded, silently impressed – not by the sage advice, but by the fact he had sung Barbara's praises to a total stranger.

Morris Cameron proved true to his word, and inside of two weeks Trent was hired and hard at work in the firm's sprawling family law division. A handful of the young lawyers and paralegals who still retained some human attributes even helped him move into a house just outside Highland Park. He couldn't afford it, but the financing was made easy when he put Johnson, Connally and King on his mortgage application. Dallas had opened up to him, a wonderland of hospitality and promise, and Trent sensed his fortunes might finally be changing for the good. He spent his remaining bankroll from Sironia to pay for a house-warming barbecue, to thank his new colleagues.

Mary Yang, a slight little attorney from the corporate division, with searching eyes and a perfect body, never lent a hand during the move-in, but she drank her share of margaritas out on the patio, swatting the first gnats of an early spring, and flicking a killer sense of humor.

Trent noticed her sweet smile, but she ignored him for the first half of the evening, and he thought nothing of it until she settled down in his single easy chair in the living room, and quizzed him for an hour about his college days. After nine o'clock, he looked up and realized she was the last guest present. She stood a while longer on the front step, chatting, and even allowed a light kiss.

Lying in bed that night, Trent wondered what was happening, and felt Fate's knife inching toward his back. All his fault, for the *bon ami* of his new friends had coaxed him to let his guard down.

He bought a Walmart atlas, turned it to the Colorado page, and left it open on his thrift store coffee table. There was more work at JohnCon – as the attorneys called it – than he ever faced at Rook and Peale, and Trent worked furiously to keep his head above water. The only Sironian he still kept in contact with was Mitch Angel, a no-bullshit private detective, the P-I he had almost suggested to Primo that day. "Find the Benedettos in Denver," Trent said over the phone.

"Things like this take two weeks," Angel answered. "When someone's just moved to town, maybe longer."

Almost a month passed before the snoop finally called back to report that Primo Benedetto had been hired as vice president of business development in the local Cattlemen's Association. Barbara was still with him, and they had bought a stately, if old, home in Evergreen. Trent listened to the report through a fog of two dozen divorce cases and worry that his roof at home might be leaking again in the spring thunderstorm.

"Here's the address." Angel recited it.

Trent thanked him and hung up, then sat waving his pen in the air, like a magic wand conjuring back the searing pain that visited him each night when he lay in bed, thinking of Barbara. Pain he had to strain to remember fully.

An hour later, he was munching chips and salsa at one of the JohnCon group's after-work appetizer gatherings at Acapulco. He was trying, and failing, to work out a Denver timetable when the seat next to him was vacated, and Mary Yang sat down. He bought her a margarita, and another. Then he took her home.

They saw each other two or three times every week. One of Trent's divorce cases actually went to trial, and he stumbled into winning the lion's share, and Morris Cameron praised his abilities and gave him a bonus. Trent put on his best suit and drove to pick Mary up to celebrate. She met him at her front door, arms folded, her famous smile nowhere to be seen.

"How long since you left Sironia?" she asked.

"Three months, I guess."

"That's long enough to get her out of your system."

"Who? Get who out of my system?"

Now Mary smirked, and her riveting gaze made him feel no better than the husband he had nailed that morning on the witness stand. "You talk about her all the time. I want you to go to Denver and either make it happen or give it up. I'm a big girl – either way, I can take it." She closed the door.

Back at his house, Trent couldn't find the address, nor Mitch Angel's written report. He called. More information had drifted in, and Mitch gave it freely, making Trent glad he had already paid the man's bill. The next morning, Trent was on a plane, trying to catch forty winks to make up for a sleepless night. Maddeningly, when he closed his eyes, he saw Mary Yang instead of Barbara.

Wednesday, shortly after one in the afternoon, Trent found Primo Benedetto in his lair – the Cripple Creek Country Club. The links outside were clogged with golfers, and Mitch had laughed about how predictable the man was: golf every week, the rich man's religion. It would have been so easy for Trent to find her in her new home, but there might be bodyguards. Besides, this time he wanted to do it right.

Primo looked up from his club sandwich. "Took you longer than I expected," he said, and kept eating.

"I have to see her."

A slow nod. "And why else would you be here?"

"I'm not kidding, Mr. Benedetto. I didn't get into this to cause you grief, but I don't think you're treating her right. And I know damn well it's illegal to keep someone a prisoner. Even a wife."

No response. Not even looking now. Trent fidgeted. He should have gone to the house. "So if you've hired some more tough guys --"

Primo waved, making Trent start, but it was only for more iced tea. He swallowed. "Maybe you're not as smart as I thought. Who's keeping who prisoner, did you say?"

Trent recovered. "Very funny, Mr. Benedetto. Tell me what a hard life you lead. I'll play a violin in the background."

"No, I'm serious." Sandwich still in hand, he leaned back. "You ever move halfway across the continent for a woman? Give up a fortune? A life? Go on, take her, if you're man enough, asshole."

Trent shifted, not sure what angle the conniver was playing now. "I'm not going to do anything to you, sir. No fistfights. No lawsuits. I just want to see her and give her a choice--"

Primo waved, dismissing him, talking with his mouth full. "Go on, I said. She's right out there, just ask her, you little shit."

"She's here?"

"On the putting green. You don't read signs? This is Ladies Day."

Trent craned his neck, saw only see blurs of light clothes through the bar windows, and he started walking hurriedly.

Benedetto called loudly after him. "And while you're at it, say hello to her new boyfriend."

Trent emerged onto a wide patio, shaking, trying to arrange his thoughts, and the creep's outburst into something sensible. It might be Ladies Day, but there were plenty of men, too, pulling on their gloves, laughing, leaning on carts, sipping bottles of beer. He moved past the driving range tees, and then he saw her, out in the middle of the crowded putting green. A tall man, perhaps three or four years younger than Trent, had his arms draped around her. But he was just the pro, guiding her through smooth strokes, saying things that made her laugh too much to actually sink a putt.

Trent made his living off of the mistakes of men with Primo's sickness – guys who went bonkers anytime another male even approached their private property. So what if the pro was being too friendly? A woman like Barbara beckoned it.

For a moment, Trent could only stand, soaking her in. The air was still chill, but her long legs extended below a knee-length skirt, and he wanted her hands wrapped around himself rather than that club shaft. His heart beat faster.

She didn't see him yet, and he took a breath. It might take a little while to convince her he had substance now, and a real future that would eventually deliver her the things she needed, but she was electric, and surely the idea of freedom— He started toward her.

She laughed again, and turned suddenly, stretched up, and kissed the golf pro, long and deep. The spring sun flashed off of something, blinding Trent. He shielded his eyes – it was an optical illusion. No. It wasn't. Their lips were pulsing suction cups, and she was smiling up at the athlete with perfect hair each time the suction cups parted. Trent scrambled backwards before their embrace ended, and tucked himself safely behind a hedge, gasping for breath.

His plane landed at DFW early that evening, and he drove straight to the apartment Mary Yang was renting while her house was being built. She smiled, and opened the door wide. Paper signs hung all around the living room, proclaiming, "Welcome Home, Trent." He stood gaping, then smiled at her.

"What is this?" he asked. "Are we back in high school?"

It would be another six months before construction on her new home was finished, and after they made love that night, he asked her to move in with him. She said "*yes.*"

Day 7

Trent's plane twisted and bucked on its roll-out, and actually skidded off of O'Hare's icy runway, the final insult that closed the airport on the last day of the Family Law Conference. Back at the safety of the airline's ticket desk, his heart was still pounding while he listened to the ticket agent's frantic offers, but the airport hotels were full, so Trent left a message on the law firm's recorder, and retreated to his home for the last two days – the Fairmont, on the lake in downtown Chicago. The delay was fortunate, he told himself, because it would give him a few more hours to look for a souvenir for Mary. Of course, she only wanted a ring.

"Tough weather for an out-of-towner, eh, Mr. Davis? Welcome back," the Fairmont concierge told him. "Yes, I'm sure, Sammy's is open this late."

Trent had his luggage sent up to the same room he had occupied all week. He buttoned up for the three-block walk to the deep-dish pizza place that had sustained him on this, and his two previous trips to the Windy City. Downtown was dazzling just two weeks before Christmas, with curtains of falling snow alternately magnifying, then muffling the holiday lights. Withering blasts of ice waited around every corner, and he took the route around F.A.O. Schwartz, expecting the famous toy store to be closed. Remarkably, its lights were still on, and through the corner door he could see its aisles crowded with people bundled up in expensive coats. A guard cracked the door and leaned out.

"You here for the benefit, sir?"

"What? No. What benefit?"

"Toys for Tots. Invitation only."

"No thanks," Trent said. "Just looking." The door closed, and something hit his leg at the same instant he heard the guard turn the lock.

"Oh, I'm sorry," a voice said. A shadow in the cascading snow. Trent looked down to see the woman who had hit him with a baby stroller. An expensive one. "Would you knock for me?"

"Jeez," he said automatically. "Won't the little guy freeze out here?"

"I've got his face covered." The shadow rolled her burden into the light, and tucked her own hair back under her hood. Pretty. Trent was smitten, then he realized –

"Barbara?"

Her mouth dropped open, and she covered it, blocking the falling snowflakes. "Oh, my God. Trent? Is it you?"

They embraced mightily, and for an odd moment, he dwelled in some other universe, hugging into the thick fur that covered her body, hungrily feeling the pressure her breasts made against his chest, even through all the layers of fabric. But a new windy city gust of air pulled him back to Earth: she had a child.

"You--" he started talking even before she gave him a peck on the lips. He pointed. "The child. Is it yours?"

"His name is Matt." Barbara beamed, as if the cold were no longer an issue for any of them. "What are you doing here?"

"Conference. Our firm works with some associates in Wisconsin, just across the border." He heard himself mumble something else about his new job with JohnCon, but his eyes never left the motionless child. "I just sort of fell into it," he said. "But who--" He pointed again.

"You have to meet him." Barbara bent down and struggled with the shroud that protected the quiet little bugger. Then his face was free, but he didn't cry, only gasped and flinched at the pelts of snow. He had dark hair, and Trent felt his stomach clench. He bent down and extended a gloved finger.

"Hey, little fella." More flinching. The kid looked doubtful, yet amazingly serene, his face all too familiar. "He isn't Primo's, is he?"

Barbara was upright, hands on the carriage's handle again. She shook her head.

"The golf guy?"

"He's yours, Trent. Trent Davis, meet Matthias Benedetto. Or Davis. I'm not sure how those things work, but I guess you are. You're a lawyer." A weak laugh, and she beamed like the cat who swallowed a whole flock of canaries.

"He can't be mine. It's been almost two years--" But his protest ended there. Matthias looked too much like every baby picture Trent had ever seen of himself.

"That's right. He's almost a year and a third. Isn't he beautiful, Trent?"

For a moment, he could only register the slow, fading beats of his own heart in its lonely, echoing cave. Primo's cryptic ravings that first day, about breeding her – they had all come true. The impossibility of it all – he chucked Matt under the chin with the icy glove, enduring they tyke's quizzical, innocent, sage-like study. He glanced up at Barbara. The child's eyes were her eyes, but neither of them held any clues that would reveal how she was capable of all this.

"Yes, he's beautiful," was all Trent could manage. "But it's freezing out here."

Barbara slid the carriage around and tapped on the glass. The guard opened the door, and smiled as if he knew her, and she shoved the vehicle partially into the warmth.

"I'm just here, seeing the relatives," she said. "Maybe we'll have a trip here at the same time, have lunch?"

"I come here a lot," Trent said, wondering – he didn't know what. "How I can I see – him?"

"We still live in Denver. I'll tell Primo you said 'hi.'"

"No. I'm coming with you. You can't just--"

Barbara's eyes darted. "That wouldn't be good. Primo's parents will be in there." Her own hands were covered with knit gloves, and she raised one and blew him a kiss. "Come see us in Denver. You look great."

And then they were in, and the guard's delighted smirk flashed the signal that Trent was not to follow. The curtains of snow didn't part until Trent stepped through the entrance of Sammy's Pizza Parlor.

When he returned to Dallas, Trent kissed Mary Yang, then moved out of her stunning new abode, and into an apartment. He had rented his own home to a young railroad executive, and wouldn't be able to reclaim it until next year. Even in the continuing avalanche of work at JohnCon, it only took him two weeks to prepare the paperwork and book a flight to Denver.

He sat across the table from Primo and his lawyer. Trent's own solicitor came highly recommended, and the man had added a couple of twists to make Trent's drafts to fit with Colorado law.

"You can have him the entire month of June, beginning when the child is four years old, Primo's lawyer said. "Until then, you may visit their home in Denver four weekends per year, as a guest of the Benedettos."

"You're not going to try anything crazy, are you, Davis?" Primo asked. The lawyer tried to shush him. "No," Primo insisted. "I want to hear it from him."

"I'll behave myself," Trent said, feeling nothing, much less fear, no matter how hard the hawk scowled. For some reason, he no longer saw Primo as the enemy. "While he's little, I'll just take him to the park, or the zoo, or whatever. You don't have to hire a guard or any of your customary shit. But when the child gets closer to adulthood, say age twelve or fourteen, he should have some choices. Longer visits if he wants."

"Of course--" the lawyer interrupted. "Mr. Davis, you of all people know those things are more properly addressed after the passage of time. Plus, if you ever move your physical abode to Denver, this can all be renegotiated."

"Your terms are very generous," Trent's lawyer said.

Trent tried to smile, wondering if this were really happening. "Yeah. It'll be nice to see both of you a few times a year. Maybe you'll let me take you and the missus to dinner."

"No." Primo slapped the table. "Forget about Barbara. She will not be present when you visit. If I have to, we'll put that in these documents."

"Not a problem," Trent's lawyer said quickly, and jabbed his pen into Trent's side. "That will not be necessary."

Trent kept the smile in place. He shook hands, and said nothing more. The wiry little hawk had aged, even walked with a limp, now. But he was still impressive. Especially after all he had endured with her.

Day 8

The ringing doorbell woke Trent, made him rise from the easy chair where he had fallen asleep. A fat brief sat accusingly on the coffee table, and the magazine on his lap fell to the floor. It was still Sunday afternoon, and when he opened the door and let in the sunlight, he had to rub his eyes to make sure that what he saw was really there.

"It's Primo," Barbara Benedetto said. Older, facial features softened by time, still stunning. She stepped across the threshold before Trent could collect himself. "He died last Wednesday."

"What?" Trent stuttered, then managed to yell the question. "Wednesday? This is Sunday. Why didn't anyone call me? Was he sick?"

Barbara shrugged, chastened only a bit. "He was old."

Trent leaned toward the door, looking for the boy, but she slammed it closed. "Where's Matt? Did you leave him in Denver?"

"Of course, silly. The au pair has him. It's still Tracy. He's totally safe." She seemed concerned only in getting her buttons unfastened, open her raincoat and let it fall to the floor. She stepped out of her heels, and stood there, arms wide. Naked.

Her lips were on his before he could speak. He barely caught her weight enough to maneuver her to the couch. He tried to ask questions, but she knew her art, and soon he was panting, face between her breasts. They moved down the hall to the bedroom, and finished with barely a word. "Just sleep for a while," she whispered.

She did, but he only lay, catching his breath and watching her. One by one, thoughts he had cast to the roadside began to sneak back into place. Primo. Was he really dead? Or was this some new device she had conjured – and for what reason? A deep impulse told him her announcement was true, and that for the first time, she was his and his alone. It was a strange feeling.

Primo – the man had turned out to be a prince. When Trent asked for a week with Matt, the old Italian gave him two. Then the fishing trip when Primo asked Trent to tag along. The old guy wasn't getting around too well then, and hired a car to deliver them and the boy to a camp in Wyoming. Primo was funny, stretched out on his lawn chair by the campfire, chewing a cigar and telling cattlemen's stories. It became one of the truly fine memories of Trent's life. But the man was paranoid to the last, and true to his word, for each time Trent arrived to pick Matt up for the flight back to Texas, Barbara had never been in sight.

The wind chimes on his back porch sang a hot, twisting song. Summer was coming, and Matt was scheduled to be here in a couple of weeks, anyway.

"How is that wonderful boy taking this?" he wanted to ask. But Barbara shifted against his arm, and one leg draped over his genitals. He didn't want to move.

Perhaps he slept, for when he opened his eyes, the shower was going full blast, and her side of the bed lay empty. Before he could rise, the water chugged off, and he watched Barbara emerge from the stall. She wrapped a towel around herself and checked the mirror, then smiled as she approached the bed. Trent found himself beckoning, and she responded, and climbed on top of him.

They made love again, and as he collapsed amid her sighs, he didn't care what happened. That she would bring the boy and all her money was a promise that flitted invisibly in the air above them, an unnecessary detail. Fate had it all in its pouch until this moment, and any tortured plans Trent had imagined for himself fell away, one-by-one, with each of her breaths.

"What now?" he finally asked. She lay, stretched out, gazing at the ceiling, playing with a lock of her own hair.

"I don't know."

"Move to Dallas," he whispered.

"Maybe I will." A sigh. "Matt needs to be closer to his real father."

"What was it?" Trent asked. "Couldn't be cancer. I never heard he was really sick."

"Heart attack. What about that Japanese girl you were seeing?"

"Mary? She's really Chinese. Just raised in Japan. Gone. Came over a few times when I had Matt. She's really great with kids. But I guess I sort of screwed that up. She's getting married in a few months."

"Why did you screw it up?"

Her casual way – that she could even utter those words, as if he were a brother, or a cousin – they jolted Trent to his core. He propped up on one elbow and looked down at her. "Why do you think? I've always been in love with you, Barbara."

She looked away. "I told you we might move back. All of his friends are in Colorado. But he's just a kid. He'll adapt."

They didn't speak for a while, and Trent didn't care. He followed the curve of her shoulder with his fingers, then touched one nipple. She gripped his hand and squeezed, either signaling for him to stop, or that she loved him. Was it four? No, five years since he last laid eyes on her. She had put on weight, but in all the right places. Was she really here?

"I forget. When are you supposed to pick him up next?" she asked.

"Three weeks. But Barbara, everything's changed now."

"No." Squeezing harder. "No, it has to stay the same for a few more weeks. He's still in school, and I want him to finish first grade in Denver."

Trent bit his tongue, fighting his deflation. "So I pick him up, just like nothing has happened? Just fly up there and get his little backpack, turn around and fly back? Will you be there, or will Tracy officiate?" It was too harsh, and he was sorry. She didn't answer.

"Barbara? Will you be there? Can't I take you to dinner, at least? Do I just have him for the month? What will you do with him, then?"

"I'll be hiking when you pick him up. It's been planned for a long time," she said. Now she turned on her side, and buried her head under his arm. "You don't have to bring him back."

Outside, the chimes came alive again. He strained, trying to hear whether she was crying or not. "Aren't we going to be a family?" he wanted to ask. Failing that, he could at least flip over onto her, pin her down, threaten her until she talked, force her to reveal the things in her past that had made her this way.

But his own history staggered around him. Could he throw stones if he lived in a glass house? He had seen her less that a dozen times in his life. That left a million days when he should have done something different. Moved to Denver. Something. Myriad chances for him to change things, to prepare himself for her onslaughts, to form the world himself, rather than let it be shaped by her sporadic eruptions. He could have spent all that time making the world better. Didn't Trent the Gladiator always fight to the death? But he hadn't.

"How often will you come see him?" It was a whisper.

Barbara raised up and gave him a peck on the cheek. "I have to go."

The Ninth Day

Mary Yang was obviously in love with Hank Nishimoto, but Trent held on to the *something* that passed between her and himself each time they were together. A feeling, a knowing, like mild electricity, every time they met in the JohnCon halls, or inadvertently touched. Too late for all that now. But Trent invited the whole firm to his place for a celebration, a sort of wedding shower. It was the least he could do for her.

Outside by the barbecue, Mary slipped her arm through his while he flipped burgers in the chill

December air. "This is above and beyond, you know," she said. "I guess I'm sorry it never worked out."

"Hush." He put his finger to his lips. "You're still the nicest female I've ever met."

"Thanks for that."

"And you're going to be happy with Hank."

"Where's Matt?" she asked, looking around. "I told you he was welcome."

"Went to the movies with his twin friends."

"OK, but I hope you'll still let him come over. Hank needs to learn more about kids --" Mary looked up, her deep eyes holding their secrets, so luscious and beckoning. The secrets he always intended to unravel. Trent promised himself he would catch her under the mistletoe before the day was over, even if it hurt.

A commotion inside the house, followed by cheers. Maybe Texas had scored a touchdown. But the back door swung open at that second, and Johnny McMillin emerged. He was overdressed in a tuxedo, already armed with a drink, though this was the first time the lead capital crimes litigator had been to Trent's house. The shapely woman he had in tow wore a bright red dress that reached halfway down her legs. Trent recognized the legs first. Barbara.

By instinct, he extended his hand, ready to play-act, as if they had been transported back into Primo's study. Barbara played it from the other extreme, instead, and leaped into his arms, and sloshed him with a wet kiss.

"Where have you been?" Trent said. "We've been calling for a week."

She giggled like a schoolgirl. "I'm here. Moved from Denver last weekend, like I promised."

Trent reeled, and from the corner of his eye, he saw Mary blanch, and back away.

"I told you the house was for sale, silly." She laced her fingers into Trent's and turned to her date. "Why didn't you tell me this was Trent's party?"

"What, you know my Colo-ray-do honey?" Johnny reclaimed her with a forceful pull. He tapped her glass with his own, then drank. "Hell, then we're one big happy family."

He turned Barbara around, and she called out over her shoulder. "Where's Matt?"

"With friends. He wants to see you."

But they were staggering off together, and Trent dreaded the act of facing Mary. She had made it easy for him by not hanging around to render her verdict. He started scraping meat off the grill.

He helped the newlyweds-to-be carry their trove of presents to the car, though his heart went to his throat each time Mary refused to meet his gaze. She stayed close to her beau, leaving no chance to clear the air, and then they drove away. Morris Cameron promised to help clean up, but only settled down in the living room with the other laggards to watch the fourth quarter, and lit up a cigar.

Trent went looking for them, and found Johnny McMillin passed out on the couch in the study. The jocks had the TV, and the paralegals had scattered in the kitchen. She was nowhere to be seen, so Trent kept picking up scattered beer bottles, until a shadow flitted behind him and he felt hot breath on his neck when he lifted the remains of the eggnog bowl.

"Hey." Barbara whispered directly into his ear. "Johnny-boy ran out of gas. Why don't we find a place to finish that?" She claimed an empty mug and raised it to her seductive, pouting lips. A smile. "Fill 'er up?"

Trent jerked the bowl away, started to set it back down, thought better, then threw it, smashing it on the floor, sending the soupy cream everywhere. Her eyes were wide, the winter color gone from her cheeks. She was shaking.

"Fill it up yourself, Barbara." He didn't look back, but stomped into the living room just as a celebration broke out. Texas had won in overtime, and it was time for him to go pick Matt up from the movies.

THE END

Hotel Purgatory
By Bull Marquette

I knew something was wrong when the redneck cab driver cussed me awake. Perhaps it was age, or early Alzheimer's, but the thick fog that surrounded us seemed to suppress any memory of just where we were supposed to be. A massive shadow came scuffing and staggering around the taxi's trunk, and I tensed up until I saw the weary face in the headlights' glare. Him I remembered, from a thousand nights like this. *Bozeman and Juarez always arrive at gigs stoned, don't ya know?* Pico must have fallen asleep, too.

"Something's weird," I said.

"Weird, hell. This is frigging bizarre," Pico bellowed. He clutched his *gitarron* like an oversized cross. "What is this place anyway?"

A red sign stained the thick fog above us, broken neon words spelling only *Hot Purg*. A shiver wriggled up my back, letting a few more bare details slip from my constipated brain. "I want to say it's somewhere in the Texas Hill Country," I said. "Looks like west of Austin. Hell, I was hoping you would tell me, old buddy."

"*Hotel Purgatorio*," Pico recited in his own language, reading letters that weren't there. "Dude, I don't like the looks of this." He lit up a joint right in front of the cabbie.

"For God's sake, put that out," I said. The driver wrestled our duffel bags to the ground, took my bills without counting, then fishtailed the cab on the gravel, leaving a void quickly filled by cricket songs.

"This is the worst dump yet, Boze," Pico said through the first blast of smoke. He spat, then a thoughtful puff. "I mean, what's up? When I went to sleep I was riding on Surefire's bus. We were booked at the Whiskey."

"Didn't rehab do anything for you?" Asking the question unearthed a certainty that we had both taken the cure a long time ago. When did we relapse?

"Don't change the subject," he said, kicking gravel. "I been playing with Surefire for four months, now. I don't remember getting back together with you, *cabrone*."

Neither did I, but all I could do was wipe heavy water droplets from my forehead and moustache, and strain to think. "Relax. If you're off the wagon, at least you have an excuse," I said. "The last thing I recall is driving my BMW on the PCH. Put that out. There are kids on the porch."

"This is a drag, man, a real drag." For once, he listened and crushed out the kernel of fire under his boot, but the small shadows scattered rather than attend our entrance. "This must be a flashback," he said. "I feel like a puppet in one of those horror movies where some demon is pulling the strings."

Pico strained to lift his suitcase, so I handed over my instrument and did him the favor. I walked quickly – ahead of him and his questions. Middle age had taught me to wait and watch, but Pico still had the mind of a child and we couldn't risk one of his rages just now, with people sleeping inside the dark monolith that loomed above us. "Be cool and shut up," I called over my shoulder. "We'll sleep it off, remember the details of the contract in the morning, do our thing and go home."

"Home? From Texas? They gonna pay us in airline tickets?" He grabbed my elbow and used his weight to pull me around, baggage and all. "If you know what's going on here, Boze, you'd better tell."

"I don't know anything."

At the registration desk, I did the talking. "Bozeman and Juarez. You know, we play guitar." I pantomimed with my instrument still in its case. "How many days do you have us booked here?" The sanguine man only shrugged, demanded our signatures and handed over some old metal keys. The lobby was one of those oak-paneled western jobs – mounted longhorns, pictures hung crooked and threadbare couches. A portrait of my career, I thought. At least the bar was brightly lit.

"That's what I'm talking about," Pico said. "Come on, maybe there's another band."

I followed, but got only as far as the cowboy-style swinging doors. When I saw the woman tending bar, I didn't dare push them open. She was late forties, probably, brown hair curly and mussed, wrinkles on her forehead that told a story of years of hard work, or worry, or both. I knew her.

"Stop, damn it." I dragged Pico back into the lobby. "Red alert. I think we've played here before."

"Bullshit."

"We had to." I was sweating for no good reason. "That woman behind the bar – I think I slept with her."

Pico peered around the doorsill, then grimaced. "Past her prime for a groupie." He dismissed me with a wave. "Go get your beauty sleep. If she's worth a damn, she's mine."

My head spiraled, like an eagle descending toward a fish, but the lake was dry. Where had I known that girl? I left her to the fumbling, awkward giant whose batting average with women was even lower than mine. But wasn't Pico married, now? Me, too, once or twice?

I shook my head, and climbed the creaking stairs. The name of that one-night stand and all of our befuddlement would come clear in the morning. Hell, perhaps this was just a bad dream, and I would wake up on the deck of my repossessed mansion in Malibu, with some luscious beauty handing me a Bloody Mary.

Deep in the middle of the night, though, a coyote howl made me jump, and when I slammed my head against the solid oak bed frame, the identity of the bargirl nuked its way out of the depths: She had to be Mousy Angie, my first girlfriend. I was ten years old, she only nine when Daddy moved me out of the Ozarks to Kansas City. That woman down there was middle-aged, but I would know those eyes anywhere.

After that, I tossed and turned, reliving my childhood with a clarity I hadn't possessed for years. Exploring with Angie down by the creek, playing jacks when there were no other boys around, riding bikes to the drugstore. We raced and climbed trees and did homework and argued and fought together. Everyone said we were two pieces of the same soul.

I lived in a tract house then, but Angie's big two-story had a garage dug into the hill beneath it. One of the garage's concrete walls had an open crawl space in it, and we would climb up a dirt-and-stone embankment and enter what we called "the cellar of dreams." There we lay in the dank cool on many summer afternoons, telling ghost stories and talking about what we would do with our lives. This was long before puberty, before we even knew what sex was.

I fought to grasp those memories, hoping I remembered my revelation in the morning. And something else – wasn't there something we discovered under her house once that was really scary? A dead animal – no, but dear God, it couldn't have been a person – That part of my memory was still fogged in, and I guess I dozed off, trying to make it come clear.

I woke in a puddle of my own sweat, but buzzing mosquitoes and hot sun couldn't stop that morning from feeling like Christmas. Who cared how we got this gig? My entire being was focused on tonight, and how I might introduce myself to my long-lost love. Maybe I would keep my face hidden, then climb onstage and start the first set with a love song to her – *Romance in North Dakota*, or *Ozark Girl*. And, by God, if she still had feelings for me – the possibilities shook my whole body as I made my way down the stairs. Pico was sitting at a table on the side veranda.

"Jesus, I drank too much," he said, resting his head in his hands. The hotel breakfast came Mexican style – refried beans dumped all over eggs and ham.

"Flush your drugs," I said. "Anyway, I remembered last night. We're both supposed to be clean."

He raised up with fire in his eyes. "And what else did you suddenly recall, *pendejo*? How did you get me to come on this trip, anyway?" The fork clattered to his plate. "I should kick your ass."

"You'll kick nothing," I said, pushing beans aside. "It ain't my bad trip. Someone must have slipped us something. Were we together at Jimmy's in Manhattan Beach?"

"Jimmy Short or Jimmy Long?"

"Jimmy Short. The crackhead." I stayed on the attack, the language Pico understood. "None of that matters. We're here, so make the best of it. Tell me about that bargirl last night." Unable to control myself, I made a fist and raised it in front of his face. "But if you say you slept with her, there'll be hell to pay."

Pico lost it and screeched his chair back. The few other breakfast-eaters – mostly old guys wearing cowboy hats – turned to watch. "You told me we played here before, Boze. I think *you* slipped *me* a mickey." He covered both temples, and his eyes rolled up. "The past is a haze, man. All a haze."

I lowered my fist. "OK, forget it. Let's both quit behaving the way that broke us up, and reason this out."

We had fought and made up a zillion times, yet just then I couldn't remember a single instance of either. "We're still best friends, right?"

He answered with a glare. "I didn't sleep with her, dude. Is that why we're here? So you can have a second honeymoon with that skank?"

Rather than take the bait, I chopped my eggs up. Before I knew it, he dragged his chair around and butted it up against mine. A glance around the room, then a whisper, "I've got another theory, man, and I'm not shitting. I was on the bus last night. I never got on some frigging airplane to come here. I ain't even seen you for almost a year."

I fought to make the eggs go down, but Pico would never understand that priorities had changed since last night. Some bad drug had given us both a taste of amnesia, but the truth would finally surface, and we could all have a big laugh about our antics. In the meantime, I was determined not to rock the boat until I had a chance to see Angie. I stalled. "That's a hangover talking. Did the barmaid say how long we're booked?"

"Shut up about that piece of tail, and put it together." He snatched the fork from my hand and used it as a pointer. "One second I'm riding with Surefire, you're in a car, both in California. Then abracadabra – Bozeman and Juarez are performing in the middle of nowhere." Close, breath of coffee and stale beer. "What if we're dead, man? What if we both just died?" He let it fly, propelled by his eyebrows, then let it lie there.

"They don't have greasy eggs in Heaven, Pico Morales Esteban. How long have you been back on drugs?"

"I ain't." Wearily, he massaged his temples again. "I just reached in my pocket and the joint was there. Let's find a phone and call Al. My cell phone don't get jack out here."

He turned, but I dragged him back down, using the remainder of my breakfast as a peace offering. "This afternoon, we practice. Tonight, we play. By then we sober up enough to remember what's going on. Fair enough?"

His glare sloughed a layer of suspicion, and I let him start eating before I whispered my plea one more time. "Now tell me about the lady."

"That bargirl? She's a royal bitch."

The hotel stood by itself in the middle of a forest of mesquite trees, coating the hills and dips as far as the eye could see. No other structures, besides a couple of out-buildings and an ancient gas pump under a canopy.

Maids and busboys traipsed to and from work on the gravel road that afternoon, but no cars, and apparently no new hotel guests. And no Angie. I watched the scattered figures drift in and out from the wide porch where children were sitting last night, sipping iced tea and strumming my guitar – how long had it been? My fingers stung as if I hadn't touched the instrument for weeks. That, plus the lack of modern vehicles out on the road made we wonder if Pico's death theory might actually hold weight.

Worse, the horseflies that swarmed us during practice out on the back lawn were no match for the butterflies in my stomach. I hadn't been this nervous since our first gig, back in college. I risked a nap late in the sweltering afternoon, jolting awake only minutes before we were scheduled to go on. On my way to the dining hall, I couldn't resist, and peered over the swinging doors. My heart jumped – Mousy Angie had arrived during my siesta, and now she was back at it, wielding longnecks, scowling at the old men who yelled orders from their ramshackle bar tables. We were so far removed from anywhere, and the lobby had been deserted most of the day. Where did all these old ranchers come from? I took a deep breath, but I wasn't ready to introduce myself yet. I retreated to a couch in the lobby until Pico found me.

"Come on," he demanded. "You can't play on an empty stomach." His hair was greased back, his soiled shirt tucked in, almost presentable.

"Can't eat," I said. "I want you to go ask the barmaid something before I make my entrance."

"Will you get off that bitch? I swear." Pico sat down, his eyebrows raised, nostrils flared. "There's no phone here. We're cut off from reality, and the *bobo* bellhops are playing dumb in two languages. I got a real bad feeling, Boze. We're either dead or in the Twilight Zone." He pulled out a cigarette, lit it and nodded toward the bar. "That woman in there, the one you want so much? She's gotta be dead, too."

I stood up, grabbed his collar and jerked him to his feet. "You're a paranoid junkie," I said. Instead of fighting back, he sneered. The last straw. "It's no wonder our career ended in shit." I pushed him away and strode through the swinging doors.

I chose a stool on the bar's short end, close enough to reach out and touch her, and my anger evaporated. Like the shabby room itself, Angie was disheveled, but she chipped away at a stubborn mound of ice with the same look of concentration I remembered from all those summers of games and philosophizing. Beauty had followed her into adulthood – long, smooth legs, firm forearms. Nothing really worn-out, yet. I could have watched forever, except that I wanted to sweep her up and kiss her.

"A beer please," I managed to say, trying to keep my heart from climbing out of my mouth. She kept chipping. "I said, a beer, please, Mousy." The nickname my mother gave her still fit – hair so curly, face and chin so delicate.

She poured a glass full of suds and slammed it on the bar without looking at me. "There. First one's free for musicians. After that, we add it to the room tab."

The cold outburst knocked the wind out of me. "Mousy – I mean, Angie, it's me, Ralph. Don't you remember?"

A grimace, but still no glance in my direction. "Go play your guitar, then get the hell out of here. You're way too late to help me now."

Three grungy cowhands on the long side of the bar were suddenly interested. The heavy-set one spoke. "Señor, you heard the lady. Take your beer and vamoose."

As quick as a puff adder, Angie popped him with a bar towel. "I don't need your help, Dirtbag. Why don't you get out, too? All of you."

Stunned, I burst out laughing. "By God, it *is* you, Mousy-girl. I'd know that temper anywhere." Under the thin cotton dress her slender body was as taught as a bow, and I was falling in love all over again. "I've missed you, girl."

"That's a lie." She turned back to her ice pick.

"It is not. I've thought about you forever. I went back through Pocahontas two or three times, but none of the neighbors could say where you'd gone." An impromptu story, but a good one. "I'll bet you've heard my songs over the years. Why didn't you look me up?"

"Me? Look you up, you lying sack of shit?" Her gaze finally locked with mine. "I don't chase little boys who break their promises."

I stuck my tongue out automatically, as if we were still kids, and wanted to follow up with a smart ass remark, but the gray streaks in her hair mesmerized me, and she leveled a wilting gaze.

"Poor old has-been," she said. "Slobbering like you want to add me to your list of conquests. Well, I'm married now, prick. Thanks to you."

My heart sank like a sad dobro riff, but the ranchers were enjoying themselves, and she returned to her tasks. Every lithe motion of her limbs, the way she shifted on her legs – how many nights had I dreamed her little girl's body into maturity, and here it was, much better than my imagination. In that instant, I decided I had come too far in space and time to let a minor thing like a husband get in my way.

"So? Being married doesn't mean you're dead." The lamest line I ever uttered. "Come over here and let's talk in private."

"Like hell," she said. "You stole a kiss once. Never again." To drive her point home, she gripped an empty Lone Star bottle and broke it against a cooler. I jumped off my stool and the ranchers retreated. The jukebox decided to change songs, and I remember thinking that if there were a God, it might have played one of mine, but I knew that even if she came around the bar, I wouldn't run. My heart would pull me back. So I opened my hands, like a delinquent waiting to be smacked with a ruler. "I never broke any promise to you, Mousy."

She stepped forward, then snorted and threw the bottleneck clinking to the floor. "You said you would always protect me, but then you left me to him, like I was nothing. Jerk."

"Him? Which him?"

Gritting teeth. "You know damned well. You moved away and let the Khot come get me."

The bar lurched beneath my splayed hands, and I was flying it solo, flashing back through decades of booze and drugs, finally landing at the boogeyman she and I used to fear more than anything, even death. That was the thing that lived in the dream cellar under her house – imaginary, of course, but even if the Khot were something we just made up, childhood spirits seem to acquire their own history.

I remembered – when she first told me the creature's name, I asked her to spell it. "It's not *cot*, like the thing you lie on, but it's spelled with a *K-h*," Angie said in her romantic way. "That makes it more mysterious, like a genie out of the Arabian Nights."

I remembered how we used to peer under her house and call out, warning that slinking, ephemeral shadow that we were coming in, and then we would climb into the cool dankness, laying claim to the territory, until it began whispering our names from behind the foundation piers. The beast/genie, whatever we imagined it to be, would sometimes let us crawl very far in, across the soft dirt, then moan right next to us, or whisper into our ears, or brush one of us on the shoulder, and we would half-kill ourselves scrambling through the dirt and gravel, crashing back out, through the hole, into the garage.

I was the creative one, and defined the creature's evil powers, drawing on fairy tales as my only guide. "If we ever let our guards down, it will scare us to death. But for whoever catches it first, it's like a leprechaun. It will tell your fortune, and give you a wish."

The memory of our old, private fable, plus the fire in her eyes, made me doubt that she was really angry. I gulped my beer. Angie had always been one for practical jokes. I was ready for the punchline.

"The Khot was something we just made up," I said, even though the hair on my neck still stood at attention. "We're grown now. Or are you talking in symbolism, Miss Spelling Bee?"

She gritted her teeth. "The Khot was real then and it's real now. You saw him that day." She jabbed a finger at me, and I feared she would go for another bottle. "Did he promise you fame and stardom if you gave me to him? After you moved away, he started calling my name from the cellar in the middle of the night, but I wouldn't go down. Then I was sick all Christmas vacation one year, and I got too weak, and he could tell, and came up through the floorboards. And were you there to protect me? No, Mr. Popular was too busy screwing cheerleaders by then."

I had no idea who told her about my high school career, but this wasn't fun anymore. "Sorry if life's been tough on you, Angie," I said. "Join the club. Maybe *Khot*'s a nickname for your problems, but don't blame them on me."

Eyes cold. "Get out of this bar."

I had broken up with dozens of wonderful women over the years, never on the receiving side, so I had never felt a sting like this. Especially from the one I always lusted after, by proxy. My heart's north star, the love of my life. But, like me, she had changed. I lifted the mug and ceremoniously poured the dregs out onto the bar.

"I'm through feeling guilty for moving to Kansas City, Angie," I said. "No, you never blamed me before now. I blamed myself. But tonight clears it up for me. We both had to grow up, girl. Sorry if you never found your Prince Charming or your picket fence." Then I slammed the mug down into the puddle I had created. "Tell you what. If you ever find that Khot again, look me up and I'll kick his ass for you"

I turned to go, and only one thing on Earth could have stopped me at the swinging doors: Angie's soft voice. "I don't have to find him," she said. "I know where he is."

"Who?" I turned. "Prince Charming?"

"No. The Khot."

The jukebox fell silent, and the ragged rounders watched from their littered tables. It wasn't hope, but despair that forced me to work up the nerve to meet her gaze again. "Yeah? Where?"

"Down in the cellar. Where else?" She pulled a baseball bat from beneath the bar, but instead of swinging it at me, she shoved it into my hands. "I'll give you one more chance to keep your promise."

She crossed the lobby and flung open a door, revealing a narrow, dank passageway. Pico had deserted me, so I dared to follow, my breath coming in short gasps. She pointed down a steep flight of stairs. At the bottom, on one side of the cement dead-end, a single bulb lit the tiny square in front of a door. For an instant, it felt like old times, and now I could expect the punchline. Then again, what if the monster really were down there? I came to my senses and grabbed her by the shoulders. "I'm sorry, Angie. Let's start this conversation over."

There was scarcely any hair left atop my head, but she took a long hank on the side and twisted it around her little finger, tight, the same death-hold she liked to use when we were kids. "Kill the Khot, like you always swore you would. Then we'll talk."

She nudged me downward, all the way to the bottom, and I braced, imagining the dank door might open up into something like Carlsbad Caverns. After all, the Hill Country was renowned for its caves. For the first time, little Mousy Angie was actually scaring me. What if she had gone mad, and just shoved me into that cavern, and I was never found?

"Angie, I can't kill a genie with a baseball bat. My God – what am I saying? Tell me this is a surprise birthday party or something."

She reached, turned the knob and swung the door open. "The Khot's in here. You can't miss him." Carefully, I took a step.

Instead of a bottomless pit, I entered a gaudily decked-out rumpus room. Electric beer signs flashed from cheap-paneled walls. A marble-topped bar and elaborate sound system filled the cellar's far end. Threadbare easy chairs and a huge couch in the middle faced the biggest TV screen I had ever seen. Amid the sofa cushions sat a behemoth of a man, munching popcorn from a tub. He glared at me across a landscape of spent beer bottles and emptied chicken boxes.

"Who the hell is this?" he asked.

"Ralph Bozeman," Angie said quietly.

"Who?" The fat man swallowed. "No friggin' way. That goddam musician you've been bellyachin' about since Day One? Sit down, Bozeman. Take a load off." He waved, a motion that made his shirt crawl, exposing even more of his fleshy belly.

I looked to her for direction. She mouthed the words, "The Khot."

"Pleased to meet you," I sputtered at the man, but my gaze didn't leave her. Sad, ridiculous reality fell into place. Mousy, my pretty little precious Angie, had gone and gotten herself married – or something – to a disgusting slob. The grinding fear deep inside my gut finally released in a rolling, huge laugh that I fought – and failed – to contain.

Her live-in tossed a rude, dismissive glance at the would-be weapon in my hand. "Ball fan, huh? You're just in time to watch the Yankees do it to your precious Angels. That's where you're from, ain't it? L.A.?"

"I live near Malibu --" I sputtered.

He didn't let me finish, but threw Angie a furious scowl. "Hey, what is this? Give the man a beer and get me another one while you're at it, you slovenly bitch. Then get back upstairs before the cowboys steal our booze."

Angie slipped behind the bar, begging me with her eyes. God, he was a creep. So much so that the laugh, still shuddering inside me, faded away, and my old protector instincts kicked in. "Hey," I said. "Don't talk to Mousy Angie that way."

"Mousy?" He sneered. "She don't go by that name no more. More like *Slutty*. Jeez--" His sudden yell made the bat slip from my hands, and I scrambled for it at the very instant that he bounced – his ass actually gaining altitude above the pillows – and hollered at the TV. "Did you see that, Punk? Cooper-boy stole another base. That's three in four innings." He swelled, and blasted out a belch forceful enough to shake the beer signs.

Angie peered from the drink well, pleadingly, and pantomimed swinging the bat, urging me toward a crime so outrageous – hell, did she really want me to kill him? When we were kids, she would pout for days if I even stepped on a cricket.

Yet, the irony, the complete wretchedness of the whole package stunned me – her being stuck in this shabby hotel in the middle of nowhere, the atmosphere of sweat that poured off of that bloated, sourpuss behemoth who shoved another handful of popcorn into his maw, even as a new blast of gas was coming out. I blinked, surveying the cheap leatherette furniture which Angie's mother would never have abided, the dark, pressed-wood paneling, the ratty shag carpet, the beer signs –

"Look at that pitch. No friggin' way," the behemoth bellowed again. "Goddam if they shouldn't kill that son of a bitch. Hey, Whore! Where's my beer?" In a movement so quick I could barely follow it, he strode toward me, jerked the bat from my hands, and held it up, menacingly. "Well, Punk? Either sit down, like I said, or get the hell out."

I was past being disgusted, and for some reason, not as frightened as a sane man would be. Rather than keep my eyes on the deadly weapon, my brain could focus only on the room's stench – hell, *his* stench. An odor of sweat and leaves and cats and lawnmower oil and stale beer. It filled my nostrils, and I clenched my hand over my mouth – though I wasn't sure whether I was holding in uncontrollable laughter or trying not to puke.

"OK, Creep," he said in a voice an octave lower than before. "I'm going to teach you to come into my home, slavering over my poor excuse for a woman--"

He raised to strike, but I was ahead of him. A right to his jaw, and two solid lefts to that marshmallow gut sent him wheezing backward. I had learned a lot in the scores of bar fights Pico and I were forced into.

A step forward, and I snatched the baseball bat away from him, wheeled around and rushed out the door before something bad actually did happen. I slammed it behind me, but it opened a millisecond later.

"Bastard," she whispered, crowding onto the stairs after me. "Aren't you going to kill him for me?"

"I – I--" I choked, and this time, the laughter fairly exploded out of me.

"It's not funny." She tugged on the weapon, but I didn't dare let it go. Then she pounded my shoulder with her fists. "Liar. I'll never trust you again."

"You call that a Khot?" I spat the words out between convulsions. "Looks more like a four-hundred pound husband to me." I cackled at my own joke, lost my footing, and wound up sitting on a stair-step, halfway up.

"Boy, and I thought I screwed my life up," I said.

She made it only as far as the second step before she collapsed, weeping.

I finally took pity on her. "I'm sorry, Angie. I was laughing because I always thought I was the one who failed. Whenever I thought of you, and imagined the wonderful places you must be going, the great causes you must be fighting for – well, never mind. I guess life dealt us both a shitty hand. For a second, I was happy when I saw your dreams had all gone to hell, too. But that's wrong. I'm really sorry."

I reached out, and took her trembling hand. "I always fantasized that you had it good, a kind husband, like you deserve. Somebody who loves you the way I always did. But cripes, killing him's not the answer. You're not a murderer, Mousy-Girl."

After a moment of leaning against the cold cement wall, she collected herself. But when I started to rise, she grabbed the cuff of my trousers and pulled – amazingly strong, like she had always been – and had me thumping down the steps on my butt until she could grab my collar.

"You always were dense, Ralph Bozeman. Didn't you see? That's the Khot in there. Don't you recognize the smell? Everywhere he goes, he smells like the mildew under my old house. I would never kill a human, or even a rabbit – but that thing in there isn't even an animal."

Tears flowed again. She shook my shoulders frantically, until she broke down. "You always said it was some horrible supernatural monster, and you were right. Now he's taken me captive, and I can never get away without your help – Did all the years of drugs rot your brain, Ralph-o? Why can't you understand?"

She really believed what she was saying. "Sure I understand," I said, "if you define Khot as a co-dependent, overbearing leech." Tears flowing down that still sweet face tugged at my heart, but I couldn't stop the giggles from returning. The whole thing was just so outrageous. I fought to be serious. "Angie, listen to me. Why don't you just divorce him?"

"Some people keep their promises."

"What? I should commit murder so you don't have to break your wedding vows?" I was suddenly inspired, and clapped my hands together, laughing again. "I've got it – if that blob's really the Khot, why not just wish him away?"

With a lightning move, she reached out and slapped my face. Lacing her fingers around my neck, she grabbed both sides of my collar again, and by the time I quit blinking, her nose was almost touching mine. "He won't grant *my* wish, dumb bunny. You're the one who caught him first."

"Hey, Boze?" Pico's voice boomed from up above. "Where the hell are you?"

"Down here, man," I cried, and staggered to my feet.

"No." Angie screamed at that instant, so loudly that it blotted out whatever Pico was telling me. "I've been waiting forever for this moment, Ralph Bozeman. Don't you dare leave. Don't you--" Again, the sobs overtook her.

This time, I touched her shoulder, trying to send all good vibes through my fingers, trying to let my feelings, rather than words, carry the message. "You always were better at life than I was, Angie," I whispered. "But I guess it finally got to you. Hey, we're human, dear one. Humans get old and die. For you and me, maybe it'll happen soon." I shrugged, and tried to infect her with my smile. "But we just gotta keep on keepin' on, girl—"

It wasn't much, after all this time, and all the things we once were to each other. But maybe the message got through, because she wiped most of the tears away, her eyes never leaving mine.

"I wish it was the way it used to be," she whispered.

"Damn, Mousy," I said. "I wish it was, too."

"Yes!" she screamed, and flung her hands up.

"Hey, Boze, goddam it, we're due on stage--"

I threw Angie a last little wink, dumbfounded at her sudden, absurd change in mood, but finding out the cause would have to wait.

"Coming," I cried, and turned to climb the stairs That's when Angie struck – She snatched the cuff of my jeans again, and pulled hard – I slipped, and this time tumbled down all the way to the bottom of the stairs.

A strange, blinding light suddenly burst into the lower hall, like a hole had suddenly opened in the center of the earth. I grabbed for her, grabbed for anything to keep from falling—

"Hey--"

But it was too late. I crashed down in an avalanche of dust and pebbles. Coughing and choking, I glanced around – the dank, mildewed hall with the stairway transformed, its walls stretching out in all four directions. My butt ached, and my eyes blinked violently in the brighter light – this wasn't the hotel, but a large room. With a concrete floor. Out in the middle of the expanse – patches of oil.

I was sitting on my ass in Angie's garage.

Sand and fine gravel rained down in a trickle, into my hair and I rubbed my rump, and looked up. Mousy Angie hovered above me with wide eyes – the eyes of a nine-year-old. The face, the body, too. She was a kid again. My heart kicked into overdrive.

"What's going on?" I managed to sputter, spitting and coughing, fighting to clear my head. No drug flashback was ever this bad – but when I worked up the nerve to meet her eyes again, she was still the little girl I remembered from so many decades ago, using little girl's hands to help me to my feet. I looked down, still brushing the dust off and, with a shudder, recognized the blue-and-tan striped shirt I had as a kid. I was wearing it.

"Did you see him?" Angie jumped up and down, her eyes alight with excitement. "You were in there so long. I couldn't find you."

"What?"

"The Khot – did you catch him?"

I stopped slapping my jeans, and flexed my hands. They looked so young. Pristine. No guitar calluses on my fingertips. No circular scar from that joint burn, no ridge of flesh at the base of my little finger from that knife fight in Peoria. I turned, and peered up into the dark hole that led to the crawlspace under her house.

"Hey, Boze," a familiar voice called again, from somewhere deep in that hole. I recoiled, stumbling until my back was against the garage door.

"What was that noise?" Angie asked, eyes wide.

I put out my hands, begging her for help. Yes, my hands, my arms – I felt my face. No beard, not even a hint of a whisker. "I dreamed I was a rock star," I said. "I had a partner. Talk to me, Angie, or I'll have to answer him."

"Answer who, Ralph? The Khot? He can talk?" Her mouth fell open. "My God, you look like a crazy man. You did see him."

Heavy footsteps resounded above us. Someone was in the house – but weren't her parents still at work?

"Don't you dare lie, Ralph Bozeman. You caught him. Did he tell your fortune, or give you a wish?" She made a fist. "If he gave you a wish, you have to share. That's the deal."

"Boze, five minutes, dude. Move your ass--" the voice called again, but softer this time, like a whisper on the wind.

I looked at her face, fearing the worst, but her wrinkles didn't reappear. Still, something pulled my gaze irresistibly back to the cellar entrance. Shadows flitted up there, and I could almost see a lonely stairway in the darkness of the hole, stifling rooms full of smoke, grueling meetings with coked-out lawyers, long nights worrying about money, and the revolving cast of women in my bed and where I might score my next high. But Angie raised her fingers in front of my eyes, blocking out those visions.

"Yoo-hoo," she said, studying me.

I grabbed her hand and blurted out the first words that came. "Mousy Angie, will you marry me?" It felt like the right, the *perfect* thing to say. But she only grimaced.

"Ralph, we're kids. Besides, how can I marry you when you're moving to Kansas City next month, dummy?"

I put my hands under her arms and lifted her up. She always hated that, but this time, she let it happen. "Not anymore. I'll get out of it somehow. That's it – I'll go home right now and throw the biggest fit of my life. Daddy'll change his mind if I make him feel insecure enough."

She looked quizzical, but before she could flinch, I pulled her close and kissed her, wondering where I had learned such sure, quick moves. A strange, awkward kiss – my lips just pushed her lips back up against her teeth – but it still felt good, and my young arms felt strong and powerful, and the blood pumped through my body, feeling fresh. And clean.

She jerked backward, out of my grasp, and I turned and ran out the side door, across her lawn, onto the street. Yes, I had to get to my house, to tell Dad, and at the same time, I wanted to stay and explain to Angie –

But none of that was important yet – an irrefutable certainty washed over me like a storm wave down in Biloxi: right now, it was vital that I put as much space as possible between me and the unholy memories that might still be able to reach into her garage.

I burst into the bright summer sunlight, those foggy images chasing me like a swarm of gnats, each one trying to take center stage in my mind – the guilt, the sorrow –

But with each touch of my bare feet on blazing asphalt, I felt the gnats melting, one-by-one.

I summoned up my nerve, and glanced over my shoulder – Mousy Angie was in hot pursuit.

"Come back here," she screamed, spitting and gagging at the end of her driveway. "Boze, I'll get you for that."

She always delighted in taking revenge. For the first time in my life, I looked forward to it.

THE END

White River Fox
By Bull Marquette

"You're a weird one," Mabel McCoy said. Or maybe her name was Mabel Clements. Robert Benoit wasn't yet sure what to call her. "Any other man would have torn my clothes off and jumped me by now."

She gazed at him from her perch on the bed. It was the first time he had ever taken a woman to a motel – Carson's Rest, Jonesboro. They had made the hilly drive from Batesville in separate cars. A long trip to escape the prying eyes of a small Arkansas town. Yet, after a quarter-hour in the room, he still hadn't touched her.

"Thought we should get acquainted," Robert said. "Sunday's usually my day to collapse. I've been delivering bread during the day and pizza at night for more than a year. I stay tired--"

"So what?" she said. "Everybody's got troubles. Tell me again about the first time you saw me."

Robert recoiled, but maybe she softened, slightly. She held out the squat hotel glass, beckoning for a refill of Chateau Aux Arc.

"The Supermart always needs a refill on Saturdays, especially garlic bread," he began, wondering what part fascinated her. "I took the route around the country club, for some reason, and turned off Fifth. And there you were, standing out in front of Butch Clements' mansion, watering the lawn."

"You drive for Rainbo Bread?"

"I told you before. Marion's Dinner Bread."

"And you thought--" She raised the glass to her mouth, waiting for him to resume.

"You looked like one of those rich crazy women, dressed up in a business suit, holding a hose. You had your stereo blasting inside, because *Moon River* was coming out of the windows. I slowed the van down – you might have seen me – but you closed your eyes, and stretched, and your dark hair fell down on your shoulders, and I realized--" He stopped. Telling her he could barely breathe by that point would be revealing too much.

"You realized I was crazy?"

"No. Beautiful. I told you the other night. If you just want to lie there and get compliments, I'll make up some more."

She gazed into her glass, grimacing. "And am I still so beautiful? Now that you know I've got two husbands?"

"I guess." The wrong answer, and Robert knew it. All week, her impossible claim had messed up his fantasies. Still, she was here, and he wanted her. Or was supposed to want her.

"Oh. That reminds me." Mabel put the glass down and fished through her purse. She brought out a compact disc in a pink plastic case, and tossed it to him. "Be a good boy and put that on," she said.

He was only twenty-five, and she might be thirty, but he ignored the down-talking, and squatted in front of the console to insert the music disc into the player below the TV. "Don't tell me. More Andy Williams?" he asked.

She returned his sarcasm with a wry smile. "It's a mix. You heard it the other night."

"No I didn't," he corrected. "Remember? Charlie made you turn the music off, right before he said your green beans tasted like crap."

"Charlie was bad that night," she muttered. "A few beers, and he don't care who's around." Another smile – this one, almost real. Andy Williams' voice started loudly, and Robert adjusted the volume.

"That's how I knew you were the same woman," he said. "This song was playing at the mansion, and there it was again, when I saw you through the door of the trailer."

Even now that second sighting gave him goose bumps. She was stretching then, too, so luxuriously, lit through the screen by the low sun's rays, like some goddess dropped down in the middle of the narrow lanes full of bawling kids, blaring televisions from cramped living rooms, and the thick smoke from Charlie McCoy's grill. Camby's Trailer Park was as far from the

Clements mansion as you could get and still be in Batesville.

Mabel sighed. "Well, there's some *South Pacific* on there, too. I like songs from back when people were innocent."

She took a long, slow sip of wine, and Robert felt a twinge, for his mother had used that same phrase more than once during his youth, when she filled the house with Perry Como, the big Broadway show tunes and Herb Alpert.

"Innocent?" he said. "Are you innocent, Mable?"

She smirked. "I was. Once." Henry Mancini's orchestra swelled, the harmonica riffed, and she closed her eyes. "And now I'm starting to feel a buzz, so go ahead and promise me you're the white knight who'll free me from my prison – two prisons – and I'll let you do what you got me here to do. Then you can disappear into the woods or wherever you come from."

"I'm not like that."

"If you're a male, then yes, you are." Another sigh, and her eyes came open, their sharpness belying any buzz. "But if your ass tries to blackmail me, I'll just confess to Charlie, and I guarantee he'll kill you before he kills me."

He never saw this hard edge in his fantasies. Only a week ago, she sat wistfully at that dinky kitchen table while Charlie cursed her housekeeping, and even called her a slut when she bent over the low sink. The glass. Again, he filled it.

"So Charlie's the alpha male?" he asked. "Is your other husband some kinda wimp? Wonder how he made millions being a milk toast?"

She actually chuckled at that, and looked around, maybe not wanting to be here at all. Or perhaps she really was looking for a white knight, and this was still the interview stage. "Butch is too old. He'd just pay to have someone else kill you."

The way she snickered, as if his punishment were a foregone conclusion, touched a nerve. Robert slammed his own glass down on the small circle of a table. "Is that what gets you off? Threatening new beaus with your old ones?"

"Is that what you are? My new beau?" Her crystal green eyes flared. She didn't need either husband to protect her. Robert was certain she could fight her own battles.

He was flustered, and took a drink. "Your dance card is pretty crowded. For all I know, you picked me up so you could talk me into getting rid of both of them. I'm an artist, Mabel, not a killer."

"I 'picked you up,' as you call it, because you sweet-talked me when you helped me take the trash out the other night."

"Maybe not a classic pick-up," he said, feeling his cheeks warming. "But here Jack and I just stopped to chat, then Charlie invited us in for dinner, and you didn't speak five words while we were eating, but you kept looking at me that way. Don't pretend you didn't. Then, when I followed you out and asked if you were the same woman watering daisies outside Butch's mansion, you confessed. Why didn't you just tell me I was blind?"

She seemed to enjoy his turmoil, and the way she tossed her head would madden the gods. People didn't go to motels to fight, but he had no idea how to break the ice. "Besides, the night was warm, and you smelled like magnolias," he said. She only looked down, flattered. Or bored.

"Maybe you're just leading me on." He pushed his aching back flush with the hard chair. "Maybe you've got a twin sister, and she's married to Butch Clements."

"If I do, her taste is a damned site better'n mine." She didn't return his gaze, but settled into the pillows.

This was going nowhere, Robert realized. All those luscious dreams of getting her out of her clothes – yes, she was beautiful, the same way a stone wall is. He would settle, he told himself, for at least finding out if she was lying. "Mabel, you can't live two lives in a town the size of Batesville," he said. "Please tell me the truth. For God's sake, explain how you do it."

Her eyes were calmer now, twinkling, the way they had looked in the moonlight by the trailer. She took a deep breath, and spoke like someone explaining math to a child. "I married Charlie and we moved here two years ago. He drives a truck every weekend – Indianapolis, St. Louis, then back to Indy, then back. Just dumb luck you and your asshole friend found him home on a Saturday."

"Jack's my boss, not my friend."

"Your boss scares me. Butch, on the other hand, sells for the casket company, Western Region, so he's flying all the time, home only on weekends. I go to his house Friday morning. By noon, Mondays, I'm due back at the trailer park."

"That's quite a juggling act," Robert said. He thought about another refill, but his stomach was churning. He reached over and turned the volume down on *Bloody Mary*. "But schedules always change. How long before their paths cross and disaster strikes? Or," the possibility hit him in the gut, "do they know about each other?"

"That's so stupid, I'm not even going to answer," she said, and closed her eyes again.

Silence returned, and Robert was tired of the verbal fencing, and out of compliments. Her face had weary lines around the eyes, and he wanted to ask if pleasing two husbands was as hellish as working two jobs at the same time, but as she relaxed, the lines smoothed out, and her arms went limp. He jumped just in time to stop her wine from spilling. He set the glass down silently, and eased himself onto the bed, still not touching her.

She slept, and he watched, repeatedly tracing the curve of her shirt collar where it strained against her cleavage. The happy sailors of *South Pacific* sang their finale. He had been one of them in his senior college play. Was she dreaming of them, or of anyone?

A couple of scheming Henry Higgins numbers followed, and Civil War erupted inside – the armies of decency battling against the waves of horniness that swelled up each time he focused on her fingers, her lips. He could take her – why didn't he?

Because of her eyes, he realized. He was thankful he couldn't see them just now, because they were dodgy, sly in a way that made his skin crawl. Then again, it would be glorious to live in those windows to her soul, just for a few days. Or a lifetime. Long enough to discover that secret knowledge, the silent longing that hovered in there like a lake ready to breech its dam.

He wanted to be the one to dynamite that dam, or at least poke a hole in it. Instinctively, he knew Charlie didn't have the power, even if he gave her rough sex, for she was holding that reservoir back for someone very special. Butch? Forget about it – that old guy was lucky to get across the street by himself. Robert propped his own eyes open and waited.

At six o'clock, the time she had insisted she had to leave, he reached out, carefully, and caressed her leg. She jumped off the bed before he could steal a kiss, slammed the door of the john and turned the water on full-blast. After long moments, she emerged with wet hair and a dazed look.

"You kept your word," she said. "I mean, about being a gentleman. Thank you."

"Can't we finish our talk, at least?"

She stopped at the door, and played with the chain lock for a long moment. When she finally looked up, her eyes held a surprising humility. "My sister," she said.

"What?"

"The girl in front of the mansion. My twin sister."

"Oh."

Then she was gone, leaving the door ajar, letting the drones of locusts and summer heat invade the dank room. He was uncontrollably horny now, but too late. He really did want her. Her sister, too. The thought made him laugh. There was no sister. She was lying. No two women could stretch that same, perfect way. Not even twins.

Landon Poteet was a deputy sheriff now, and card nights had gone downhill ever since Boxer invited him in, because the guy was born with a poker face. Robert never liked him in high school, anyway. Too mild-mannered, with a soft, grating stutter he hadn't outgrown, assuming you could ever get a word out of him.

"Well, what about it, Robert?" Boxer said loudly.

Robert threw the cards in. "I fold."

Boxer slapped the table. "Not that. I meant grad school. Did you get accepted or not?"

"Heard yesterday. I'm in the top four."

"Top four?" Tom howled, though his gaze stayed on the cards in his hand. "Sounds like our boy's moving to Connecticut."

Robert took a swig of beer, wishing he were walking down by the river with her, instead of here. "You bozos, I told you a hundred times," he said. "Yale accepts only one candidate into the degree every year, so you might be stuck with me."

"What the shit kind of degree is it?"

"Dramaturgy," Landon answered for him, nailing the word in three tries. Three quiet tries. "History of the theater." He beckoned for two cards. "You eight balls don't hear much, do you?"

"Thank you, Deputy," Robert said. Catcalls started from the other two, but Landon held up a finger.

"A lawman's gotta have sharp ears," he said. "Poor Benoit is just dyin' to escape the small town trap. I tried to get out once, myself. Ain't so easy."

Boxer laughed. "Going to police academy in Little Rock for six weeks don't exactly qualify, Poteet."

Tom moaned, and shook his head. "Dream on, bastard. You'll never get out, because you can't go goddam fishing on Broadway. Remember when we used to trap rabbits in grade school?" He poised his hands in the air, then slammed them together. "Snap. See? The White River's got you for life, boy. We're all stuck in these hills. Theater sounds like a fag subject, anyway."

"Oh, hell, I knew Bobby was a fag from that time we snagged a fox, and the dumb shit let it go," Boxer said. "We coulda got at least fifty dollars for it."

"No shit? Why'd you let it go, Robert?" Landon asked.

"'Cause we couldn't eat it." Robert shot them the bird, and studied his cards. But, he remembered, the real reason was the way the animal looked up at him – pitiful, sorrowful, as if it blamed itself for stepping into that crate for a tiny morsel, when it knew better. Like a coyote, a fox's eyes hid lies too quick to catch, but on that greasy afternoon so long ago, Robert discovered foxes were fallible, too. And that poor thing begged him with those shifty eyes, so he broke the slats and the sleek creature darted off into the forest.

"It was my trap," Tom said. "So that woulda been my fifty dollars."

Landon laid his cards open, and took the pot. Robert stared at him, and the question simmering inside came to a boil, even before he was ready to voice it.

"Hey, Poteet," he asked, "what if a guy saw a crime being planned, but had no evidence yet? When should he go to the police?"

"What kind of crime?"

Boxer was dealing, but their gazes drilled Robert, and he was sorry he'd said anything. "Hell, I don't know," he blustered, not meeting their eyes. "Robbery, maybe murder. Or maybe just bigamy."

"Bigamy?" Boxer guffawed and the others joined him.

"Who're you talking about, bastard?" Tom asked.

Robert finished his beer, and stomped toward the cooler, making up an outlandish scenario as he went along. "Over in Collierville, the other day, some barflies were bullshitting bout some woman with two husbands. She lives in two different towns, and the two studs don't know about each other. Their theory was that she's gonna kill the rich husband, take his dough and run off with the younger one."

The others glanced at each other, but Landon seemed intrigued. "She don't belong to that nudist cult up around there, does she?" he asked. More laughter.

Robert shrugged. "Well, if something does happen, I just wondered if those who knew about the situation would have any liability."

"Well, duh," Tom said. "One husband's bound to find out, and shoot the other guy and her. Go sic 'em, Poteet."

Landon giggled, and spoke in his near-whisper. "Why don't Robert just get us that slut's phone number? Maybe she needs a few more husbands."

They stomped the floor, and clapped, but Robert sank back into his chair while the cards kept dropping. These yokels were the rabbits in the trap. But they would never understand that traps weren't fashioned by small towns, but in people's own hearts.

No doubt, Mabel made her own prison -- fell in love with McCoy before she knew what a creep he was, and now was caught in some awful plot the loser dreamed up. "I'm done," he said, and tossed the cards. He wouldn't push his luck any further – let Fate decide if their paths had really crossed. Then again, he knew where Mabel lived – both places.

Early the next week, Yale demanded one more essay. Robert pulled out his books, researched, and wrote it about names. There was a famous Mabel in *Pirates of Penzance*, but none of Shakespeare's heroines wore the moniker.

Each time he delivered to the Supermart, he passed the mansion. The windows were shut tight, no Fifties show tunes seeped out, and the front rooms lay dark and empty.

He scrawled Butch Clements' phone number on the back of his order book, even took his van on detours to the trailer park. But an inner voice kept him from dialing the number, or passing through the gates. *She's damaged goods, twice over*, it said. If love at first sight were possible, why couldn't it happen again with any of a thousand women at Yale? Maybe the guys were right. Every day he spent here, he risked being trapped.

On Wednesday afternoon, he was stooped over, fronting-up loaves in the College Shop, mentally rehearsing how he would give his notice to Jack – whether Yale took him or not – when a tartan skirt brushed against him.

"I knew I should have gone somewhere else," the woman said, and laughed. He looked up, directly into Mabel's crystal green eyes. A deep shudder – this was the sign he was waiting for. The fourth ace falling. A call out of the blue from a casting director. He felt suddenly brave, maybe even immune to her charms. So he played it cool.

"Is that you, Mabel? Or maybe her sister, Maybelle or Agnes, or whoever you are?"

Instead of biting back, she laughed. "How long did it take for you to figure it out?"

"About thirty seconds," he said. Her skirt looked somehow expensive. Not the kind of tartan you would see in Camby's Trailer Park. "I also figured out your scam. You and that Charlie character are going to hoodwink poor Mr. Clements out of his fortune. You gonna marry him or kill him?"

For an instant, she seemed surprised, but then the wry smile returned, and she leaned against the shelves of peanut butter and honey. "I already married him. But that's not what you're thinking right now. You're wondering if this ain't karma, us running into each other again so soon. A sign from God. You're hoping this might be your ticket to finally get into my pants. Admit it, Robert Benoit."

He shook his head, fighting her irresistible wave. "You're not wearing pants, and this is the middle of the week. Aren't you supposed to be with Charlie?"

She shook her head. "You always appear on off-days, for some reason. Butch had meetings at the company all week. Tonight's my first night to entertain the bigwigs."

"And Charlie's just sitting home? Oh, yeah, he's in on the scam, right?"

"Smart ass." She grabbed a package of rolls, seemingly at random, and tossed them into her basket. "I threw a fit until he took an extra trip. Good ol' Charlie's probably in Des Moines right now." She paused, and he felt like a helpless fish being reeled in by the quiet allure in her eyes. "Tomorrow, Butch leaves, so it all works out. I'll just have time to get back and clean up the trailer, 'cause Charlie's back Friday morning."

Was this an invitation? She wasn't the type to come right out and say things. "So the juggling act gets more intense," he said, and pushed his dolly into line next to her basket. Together they rolled toward the dairy case. "I wish I knew how this ends, Mabel. You can't keep up this ping-pong game forever."

"I guess you'll just have to stick around to find out." She pinched his cheek, then turned away, down the soup aisle, throwing her hips as she did. Long days of trying to get over her went right out the window.

"You're right about one thing." He said it loud enough to stop her. She turned, and he whispered, "I do want to get into your pants."

Thursday, the air hung hot and heavy from the trees, so wet you could taste it. The riotous kids were silent – oh, yeah, back in school by now – but the never-ending buzz of the locusts pulled all hope out of the soul of the trailer park. Robert crunched along the gravel paths, catching occasional glimpses through flimsy windows of old women and men wearing expressions as forlorn as the atmosphere, imprisoned behind the pumping of their dinky air conditioners.

She hadn't answered the door at the mansion. So now he tried to retrace the steps he took when Jack brought him here. Down the boat ramp to the river, then back up, tacking through narrow lanes and alleys, hoping he would recognize the McCoy trailer in broad daylight. He was due at the Friendly Mart in Moorefield, and this detour had already added thirty minutes to the trip.

Suddenly – *jackpot*. Behind a miniature picket fence, he spotted the barbecue where Charlie McCoy had stood raining lemon juice down on catfish filets while Jack greeted him like an old friend. He also recognized the thick fishing net that hung over their front porch. From it hung sea shells and nautical doodads like starfish and fishing lures. In the sunshine, the decoration reeked of rotting hemp. The trailer windows were as dark as the mansion's, but Robert fingered a petrified seahorse, working up the courage to knock. In that same instant, the aluminum door slammed open. There stood Charlie, himself, hoisting a plastic trash bag.

"Huh? That you, Benoit?" The man's paunch filled out a white wifebeater, the same kind he wore on that first night.

"Hello, Mr. McCoy."

"What the hell you doing here? As if I didn't know." He laughed a sick little laugh.

"What do you mean by that?" Robert's heart slammed. But it sank, also. Did Mabel lie only about her changing schedules, or about everything?

McCoy dropped the bag on the gravel walk. "Don't play dumb, Boy. Mabel said you were on her scent."

"That's a lie." He had no fallback – he hadn't expected this. "Came here to see a friend," he said, weakly.

"Uh-huh." McCoy lit a cigarette, stuck the lighter into his pants, and in almost the same motion, produced a pistol from behind his back. Robert retreated, tripping over the short fencepost, but McCoy was quicker, took a long step, and dug the weapon's muzzle into Robert's midsection before he could even straighten up. Large-bore. A forty-four at least.

The air left Robert's lungs. Close-up, McCoy's sweat smelled worse than the hemp. This scum would respond only to strength, so Robert tried. "You can't shoot me in broad daylight, Mr. McCoy."

"Hell, I can't. This is a free pass." McCoy pulled him close. "Mabel'll testify how you raped her, and they'll let me off." He slid the gun up Robert's chest, smooth and easy until it came to rest against his head. "Even your buddy, Jack, told me you wuz slobbering all over her."

"That's a lie," Robert said, shaking from his feet up. "Jack doesn't know shit. Mr. McCoy, if Mabel's sleeping around, I'm not the guy--"

"Shut up. Don't say her name." The lout's eyes brimmed with tears, and he took short, violent puffs on the weed. "Let this be your only warning, Punk," he said.

"I'm watching you close. And I have friends. Don't come around her again. Is that clear?"

"You don't know what she wants in life--" Robert started, but saw his only chance, and took it. He turned and jogged up the rise, ducking into the first side street he crossed. At the park's gate, he was so winded and shaking that he almost didn't dodge the car that approached. Mabel leaned out of the driver's window.

"Robert. My God, what are you doing here?"

"He's here," he gasped. "Not Des Moines. You lied."

"He blew in last night. Don't you know better--"

But Robert ran for the bread van, and reached Moorefield an hour late.

"I've got a present for you."

Robert was gulping his lunch in the van, parked behind the Crunchy Burger. He laid his lunch basket on the floor, and tried to remember when – or if – he gave her his cell number.

"Robert?"

"Mabel, you're a liar. I'm sorry you've gotten mixed up in whatever that McCoy bastard's got planned, but I don't want any part of it. I'm not a home wrecker, anyway."

Quiet on the other end. For too long. "Both my homes are already wrecked," she finally said. A long pause. "You've gotten under my skin, Robert."

The words hung there, and he didn't respond, but she recited directions to the Star Bridge Motel in North Little Rock. Another long drive, and for what? "Charlie was so mad that he piggy-backed a weekend trip. Please, Robert. I'll be free all night, and it might be my last chance."

Hours later, they met in the motel parking lot. She had already checked in, and started spilling answers before he could ask. "This was the closest call yet, but now Butch won't be back from Los Angeles until tomorrow night. For once, we have time to be --" She didn't finish.

In the room, she took off her quilted jacket and tossed it across the chair. He closed the curtains and the air conditioner came on with a roar. She clutched her purse in front of her like a shield.

"Mabel, did he beat you?" Robert began. "I thought I was a dead man."

"That's why I brought you this. Close your eyes."

He wasn't quick enough to prevent her from pulling a pistol from the purse, and laying it across his hands.

"What the hell are you doing?" He jumped back, letting the weapon dangle from his finger and thumb.

"His gun. Now, it's yours. Didn't you accuse me of planning to murder Butch? Why don't you use it to get rid of both of them?" She smiled slightly. Eerily.

"Are you crazy?" His gut clenched so hard, he could scarcely take a breath. Gold glistened behind the revolver's cylinder. "This thing's loaded." He threw it down on the bed. But when she reached for it, he panicked, and snatched it up again. He flipped the cylinder open and dumped the shells onto the spread, then scooped them up, shaking so hard the bullets rattled in his palm.

"What the hell's wrong with you?" he asked.

She sank to the bed, and stared into his eyes for a long moment. "I'm in a trap," she said. "My fault, I know that." Maybe she was lost, or just frightened. He studied her, and still couldn't find anything evil in that gaze. She reached out to touch his fingers. "But then someone like you comes along," her voice, soft, "and it doesn't seem possible. I keep trying to put you into a category, but I can't."

"I'm in the category of *this isn't going to work,* Mabel. Whatever fix you're in, murder won't get you out of it. I look at you and see something enchanting, a woman I want more than anyone I've ever met, but then you do something stupid, like this. Something tells me you're still taking orders from that sicko, Charlie. Is that it?"

He pocketed the shells, though, and wiped his sweaty hands on his jeans. She put the weapon back into her purse, then maneuvered him to the bed, and sat on his lap.

Whispering now, into his ear, "Sometimes I think you're just after sex, like the others. But then I realize you might really like me." A tiny, butterfly-like kiss. "Forgive me for not knowing what love is, Robert. I've never felt it before."

"Are you sure it's not just panic?" he asked. "Tell me now, no bullshit – what are you and Charlie planning?"

But she pushed him, until they were both down on the flat plane of the hard motel mattress. Her kisses grew in power, and he tried to endure them like stage kisses.

But slowly, that force that had lain in wait ever since the first day he saw her, came awake.

They made love, showered together, and when they emerged, she crawled back under the covers without prompting, and melted into his arms like a frightened soul seeking refuge. Had the real Mabel emerged from her shell?

"What if you can save me?" she whispered, reading his thoughts. "You gonna just deliver bread all your life?"

"Going to grad school, if you're really interested. I almost have enough money saved. I'll know next week if I got into Yale."

"Yale?" The way she laughed, he might have announced he was running for the senate. Then, quietly, "That's what I want, too, to move far away."

"Come with me."

"What would your girlfriend say?"

"Don't have one right now. If you turn me down, I'll just have to get lucky with some Ivy-leaguer." Stupid to say that to any woman. He tried to recover by pulling her close. "Get however many divorces you need, and come with me to Connecticut. When I graduate, I just might take you to Hollywood."

For a moment, maybe she considered it. But rather than answer, she pushed into him. She fit perfectly.

He awoke at ten, in pitch darkness, and her voice sounded shaky. "It's late."

"You said he wouldn't be back tonight." He gripped her wrist. "Or were you lying again?"

"No." She ran her fingers through his hair, and pulled him close. "Just remember that I like you, Robert."

Alarm bells. "What's that supposed to mean?" he asked. She didn't answer, but urged his hand to rove and responded to every touch, until she pulled him, wordlessly, on top of her. This time, it was glorious.

In the morning, her side of the bed lay empty. Nervously, he searched the room. The bullets were still in his pants, along with his cash – all of it. At the front desk, another revelation: Mabel had already paid the bill.

Robert smiled, and steered his car onto the highway. He had had enough foresight to trade shifts, but was already late. That didn't really matter anymore, did it?

When Robert came through the back door, Peterson looked down from the loading dock, shaking his head like someone who knew well the grief of getting reamed by Jack. Robert gave a thumbs-up, anyway. Getting fired right now would be a blessing. But something seemed wrong when he stepped through the door. Instead of a simmering volcano, he found his boss leaning back in his chair, pale, and slow to react.

"You know Landon, don't you?" Jack said.

From the corner of the cluttered office, Landon Poteet smiled. "You gotta come with me, Robert," he said. "Sheriff Johnsey is pretty damned hot. Hell, I thought you had the morning shift. Missed you at poker last night, too."

"What are you talking about?"

Maybe Landon was too slow, because Jack interrupted. "They found Charlie McCoy down by the river in the middle of the night. Shot dead. Can't find his wife anywhere. Somebody said you two had words. Did you kill my friend, College Boy?"

Robert was sitting in back of a patrol car before he started to understand. At the station, a man in a suit asked questions, but seemed uninterested in the answers. Landon sat in the corner, his eyes shifting whenever Robert glanced his way.

"Why did you do it, Bob?" Landon asked, after the man left.

"I didn't." He clasped his hands together, trying to stay under control. "Maybe she did. She had his gun. You've got to help me."

"Can't find his wife, Bobby. Where'd you leave her?"

"Damn it, she's the bigamist I told you about. I just changed the players." Robert strained against the cuffs that held his hands behind him. "She was married to that McCoy guy, and old Butch Clements at the same time. Go check his house, she's gotta be there."

A new pair of cops invaded the room before Landon could respond. Any bail would certainly be denied, the big one threatened, pending the discovery of the body of Mabel McCoy.

They took him down the hall and parked him in a cell with only a concrete bench to lie on. An hour later, they pulled him out, and re-convened in the interrogation room. A court-appointed lawyer named Jasper Fink appeared, short and slight, wearing a seersucker shirt under his coat. Fink didn't say much, but scribbled notes each time Robert repeated his history with Mabel.

Maybe it was midnight – Robert had lost all track of time – when Sheriff Cliff Johnsey, himself, appeared in the doorway. His shoulders were almost too broad to fit through, and when he looked down his nose, Robert almost doubted his own innocence.

"Let's cut the bullshit," the big man said. "Your jeans tested positive for gunpowder, the right caliber bullets were in your pocket, and your goddam prints were all over the murder weapon. Charlie McCoy is dead, and where is his wife, you son of a bitch?"

"I've been telling them to check out Butch Clements. I thought they were conspiring against *him*, but I had it backwards." He watched to see if his words had any effect.

The big man fumed, but Landon leaned forward on his stool. "Bobby, you picked a bad alibi. Mr. Clements is one of the sheriff's biggest campaign contributors."

"That don't mean shit," Johnsey said, and waved Poteet back to his corner. He hovered over the table, staring Robert in the eyes. "Maybe you read in the paper how Mr. Clements moved away this week to California, to market that new battery his boy invented."

Robert choked, and the sheriff seemed to enjoy that. "Maybe you thought we'd let you out while we chased my old pal all over creation. Give you time to vamoose, huh? But why drag his wife into it? She's a real lady, you bastard, not a bigamist. I attended their wedding." A nod. "Poteet'll tell you. He was there, working security."

Landon stuttered with his eyes, so the sheriff answered for him. "Butch Clements met that pretty little thing in Branson last year."

Robert jumped to his feet, forgot his wrists were shackled to the table, and came crashing back down. "Then show a picture of that pretty little thing around the trailer park," he bellowed. "Better yet, you both know what she looks like. Find a photo of Mabel McCoy in their trailer. It's the same friggin' woman, I tell you."

Johnsey turned to one cop, then another, but Landon delivered the verdict. "Didn't find no pictures in the McCoy place at all," he said.

Gazes turned back to Robert. Quaking, he put his hands together and begged. "Get Clements to fly back here. I'll pay. Got money saved for school. For God's sake." He began rattling his story all over again, until Johnsey's fist came down on the table.

"Goddam it, son, don't make me drag the river for that woman's body. I'll give you one hour to confess."

Fink, the lawyer, scribbled, but Landon stepped forward and unlatched the chains. More cops clustered around, and when they reached the hallway, all the waves broke at once, and Robert started weeping.

"I didn't kill anyone." He tried to jerk out of Poteet's grasp. "Tell him, Landon. You've known me forever."

An electronic buzz popped a door open, but Robert twisted free, and fell through the blue suits, onto the floor. "It's the same woman," he cried. "She's always playing *Moon River*. It's her favorite song."

Rather than grab him, Landon waved the others away. "What'd you say?" Then, over his shoulder, "Hear that, Sheriff?"

The big man boomed out of the doorway like a thundercloud. But something burned in Landon's eyes, and he finally sputtered it all out. "Think back, Sheriff. At the wedding, the bride insisted they play Moon River instead of the wedding march. Those society women were scandalized. Remember?"

Robert's heart leaped, and Johnsey stopped in the middle of the hall. Slowly, the big man pulled a tin of Copenhagen from his hip pocket, and removed a pinch. "So? This boy's in grocery stores all the time. Maybe he overheard those same old biddies talking about it," he said. "Lock him up 'til he's ready to tell us where we can find Mrs. McCoy."

They shoved him down the inner hall like a town drunk, back to the tiny cell. The stench of the place made him wretch, but he held it in, wiping his tears, and straining to think of any more clues that might free him. His thoughts only assembled, swirled, re-assembled and settled into the same rut. My God, this was a terrible injustice – but then again, she had warned him, hadn't she?

The door buzzed shut, not the sound of a cell door, but a springing trap. When Landon turned away, a white light glinted off his badge, and Robert remembered the music disk. He jumped to his feet.

"Wait," he cried. "I know where it is --"

Landon's face fell. "The body?"

"No. Carson's Rest, in Jonesboro. I took her there a couple Sundays ago. We left her CD in the player."

"So?" The poker face remained. "Having an affair with Mrs. McCoy just incriminates you more."

"It's her CD, Deputy. It starts with *Moon River*, and it has to have her fingerprints."

Looking down, kicking his black boot against the bars, Landon looked as helpless as Robert felt. "Hell, the next guests probably just took it rather than turn it in," he said. He was right, of course. The cell's bars never seemed thicker.

Then the truth crashed in – so obvious, every one of these yokels had missed it. Robert reached out and grabbed a sleeve. "Fingerprints, Landon. Hers'll be in both houses."

The deputy blanched, and Robert felt every inch of his soul being searched, until suddenly the poker face broke – with the very slightest of smiles. "Prints, eh? I guess it would take a lot of work to rub down both houses," he said. A deep breath. "I'll check them out."

Robert collapsed onto the metal bed, his body shuddering as every emotion in the last twenty-four hours self-destructed in a blazing fever. He tried to remember Mabel's face, but her eyes were that trapped fox's eyes. Their message traveled down through all those years – *foxes are smarter than rabbits*, they said. He sank down, onto his knees and prayed for the first time in years, prayed that this fox hadn't thought of everything.

THE END

The Sign
   By Bull Marquette
      Inspired by an astral-traveling episode of
      Robert Monroe.

Brad entered the shopping plaza from the east, through the picturesque maze of tall hedges, pathways of thick, well-trimmed holly that separated the back offices from the rest of the plaza. The first layer of security. After escaping that, he had to endure the jaded gazes of Marilyn Rogers' guards, their electronic probes and even frisking, though Brad had been here so often, they usually just waved him through.

Such familiarity was hard-won, the product of a long, discrete cultivation that entailed learning techniques of selling, studying chemical interactions and memorizing encyclopedias of technical data. Only with patience had Brad become Marilyn Rogers' closest confidant.

"You have performed the first part of your mission brilliantly," High Priest Ferdinand had said.

"Now comes the end game: getting rid of the richest woman in the Universe."

Sweat trickled down Brad's temples, but he pasted on his customary smile for the guards, and kept his hand away from the shell in his pocket. A simulated seashell, so perfectly counterfeit that, should they discover it, they would not know its evil capacity.

"Good afternoon, sir." Archibald the butler pointed him up the stairs, and Brad tried to look casual as he wiped the drops of moisture from his brow. Today was a dry run, supposedly. They made him take the shell just in case an absolutely perfect opportunity presented itself. After all, even an arch-heretic like her deserved one more chance to recant.

From down below the tasteful second-floor entry veranda, the candle shop's spicy scents and the garlic pangs from the snobby restaurant were supercharged on the chill autumn air. From this higher vantage point, he could see the hodge-podge of stores issuing their bustling shoppers.

He stood there, mesmerized, as one of the lithe, over-coated female bodies down there did a certain turn, and raised her hand in a friendly gesture – from this distance, it could have been the ghost of Francine, on her way to holiday shopping in Shelldrake's Department Store. The stylish ghost gripped the arm of one of her girlfriends, and threw her head back and laughed, her loose skirt billowing in the happy breeze in front of the bookstore. Another echo of Francine. Brad looked away.

He took a grounding breath, knocked on the leaded glass door and waited. The next-to-last time he would ever do so, if the Priests had their way. Brad recited his price-points, features and benefits silently. How nice it would be to simply reap the benefits of his cover story: make the sale of the exotic substance he was purportedly here to sell, collect the astronomical commission and retire with impunity.

A rustling inside. A voice. Marilyn Rogers, no doubt calling to her disgusting pet. Some said Marilyn was one hundred fifty years old, others said two hundred eighty. Supposedly, she had bought the fountain of youth, anyway, and could make it to five hundred eighty, if she chose. Why the rush to end it now? Why not let her live and give the next generation of holy men someone to fight, too?

"Brad, you're a vagrant. A rotten bum for not calling me in three months." Marilyn flung the door wide open. "I was about to engage another metallurgy firm."

"Don't you dare. You don't know who you're dealing with." He boomed his voice, and they both laughed. As if *he* could threaten *her*.

"Were you followed?" she asked, as she always did, handed him a goblet and poured wine.

"Me? Those muckety-muck preachers won't put a tail on me unless they want to learn some new curse words."

Irreverence never failed to send her into gales of laughter. Espionage and stealth would not work against the Grand Dame, anyway. It wasn't a matter of discovering her modest apartment – everyone knew where she lived. The trick was piercing the layers of government assassins, satellite recons, mobsters, psychics and even evangelists who protected her, a defensive mechanism too daunting for the Temple-masters to dare test; thus they refrained. Until now. The shell-weapon chafed in his pocket.

She guided her stout form toward the settee and Brad sat in the chair opposite, but not before remembering his manners. "Hello, Barnaby." He waved at the sizeable taxidermied Dalmatian in the corner. At the same instant, the building was rocked by a loud *boom*. He grabbed her wine glass just as it threatened to topple.

"Goodness. That was a big one." Marilyn sighed, but her attention was on her former pet who had lived to the ripe old age of forty, thanks to expensive immortality treatments. "Poor Barn. Such a good dog." She wiped a tear, demonstrating that her own recent tear-duct transplant had taken. The number of youth-giving operations she had endured and even her true age were facts Brad's extensive research had failed to uncover because the Priests had expunged so much of the record. Their paranoid, restrictive methods rendered them their own worst enemies.

She accepted her rescued goblet from his fingers, and a flash of orange across the floor made them both start. "Oh, there he is. Twinky, Twinky."

Brad was on his feet, a shiver coursing up his spine as it always did when he glimpsed Marilyn's other pet – this one still living – a Firecat from the boiling Sea of Reeds on Venus.

"Pretty baby." Marilyn clucked and talked baby talk to the wiry quadruped whose fur glowed as brightly as a flame. Just a little more than foot tall, the swift, long-bodied beast slinked rapidly from one piece of furniture to the next, pausing behind each one just long enough to peer at Marilyn and her guest with eyes Brad had never grown to trust.

"That's right, baby," she said. "Ol' Barnaby's gone, and that means baby gonna have to inherit all of Momma's fortune by hisself, won't he?" She petted the writhing feline-like thing and winked at Brad. "You don't have to pretend, Dear. I know you think Firecats are thieves and debaucherers, but I would trust my life with Twinky."

"It's not that, Marilyn--"

A dismissive wave shut him up, and she lifted her gold telescope, stood up and aimed it out the window, even while she nudged the creature away with her foot. "On Venus, they say these little devils are smarter than humans," she muttered, a cliché she never failed to utter when the scurvy little monstrosity was around.

Twinky zipped into the hall, out of sight, and Brad sank back down in his chair. From this lower vantage, he could see little black specks dangling in space, near the Sign. Pretty damn big blast-ships to be so visible. This latest explosion, like every blast so far, appeared to have done absolutely no damage to the Sign.

"Ha, ha, you bastards. You can't even scratch it." She clapped her hands and stopped beside Brad on her way back to the couch. "How many mega-tons of nucleum have they wasted trying to bring my masterpiece down? Have the government quants ever figured that? Hell, persecuting me is the number one cause of this recession."

She gripped Brad's chin, turning his head toward her. For an instant it seemed she might kiss him. Marilyn was old, but sex was still in her lexicon. Or so the stories went. Youth potions, again. And Brad wasn't ego-less. Many times he had imagined what it might be like to seduce her, become her companion – escape the priesthood and their murder plots. Maybe even supplant the firecat for the greatest inheritance in the history of the Universe.

Marilyn smiled sweetly, raising her glass in a toast to the Sign. "They can't damage it because Brad's firm is the finest construction outfit in the galaxy." A motherly squeeze of his shoulder, then she plopped back down into her cushions.

He played for time. "Halloween's just around the corner. Why aren't the shops down there decorated for the holidays?"

Instead of replying, Marilyn seemed lost in thought until she raised her glass again, this time in the direction of the large portrait above the mantel. "To my son."

"Hear, hear. Cameron Rogers." Brad bowed his head, then downed the wine. She was quick to pour another.

"Poor dear," Marilyn said, collecting herself. "You're in financial distress and this is your own season of hurting, isn't it? How many years since you lost Francine, my darling?"

"Ten." His fingers played on his leg, inching near the hidden shell. Keep your hand away from it, he scolded himself. Bide your time.

"Only one-tenth as long as my Cameron's been gone." Marilyn sighed, raising her glass yet again. If he tried to match her drink-for-drink, he was a dead man.

She kissed the air between them. "Still, the pain never ends, does it? You are so much like him. If he had lived, if I had seen him hurting as you do, I might have built the Sign anyway. Perhaps it was my destiny to build it."

Brad laughed. "You honor me, Madam. Don't worry about my finances. Business is bound to turn around next year."

"Don't lie, Bradley. I have my sources. Himmel Gesellschaft is losing customers because you are affiliated with the lady who built the Sign. The three firms who participated in the greatest construction project in the history of the Universe are now having trouble landing new contracts. What irony." She sipped.

Brad shrugged and laid out his sample book. Getting into this conversation could keep him here all night, and he didn't trust the shell in his pocket, no matter how inert the scientists had promised it to be. It would be no great surprise if they had it wired to take him out, along with the Great Lady.

"Getting down to business, Brad-y? Always duty first with you, eh?" Her rich voice broke his shaky reverie.

"Yes, Ma'am."

Her hand moved toward the sample book, but found the wine bottle, instead, and executed yet another refill. "Now, let me see what sort of finishing lacquer for my Sign your research boys came up with."

He watched her flip through the samples, acting properly impressed with each new alloy Himmel's scientists had devised, though her understanding of building substances surpassed even theirs. She knew all the possible combinations, from mud to sonic water bricks. Some said she created the Sign's core alloys herself. Others claimed she hired a genius to make them, then buried him in the structure's magnetic foundation.

"Tell me again what this tricky mercury is supposed to do." She tilted her spectacles to read the captions, but Brad's fingertips returned irresistibly to play along the contours of the weapon in his trousers.

He could feel its ridges, each of which contained enough energy to power the entire planet for a month. The devilish device had never been used before, never even been tested. It would not knock down the Sign, nor kill Marilyn completely, but that was all the armaments division would divulge about the weapon's effects.

"But what does it do?" he insisted of Friar Botelli. "Shoot her with a laser or something?"

"It meets out heavenly judgment, what else?" the crazy priest had made holy signs in the air when he answered.

High Priest Ferdinand was more forthcoming. "What it will actually do is above your clearance level," he had said. "The punishment it inflicts will be appropriate for a woman who dared to mock the Universal Faith so blatantly." Brad moved his fingers away. The thing had only six clicks in it, and if he punched it by accident, he was confident he would not be around to use the other five.

A sharp tap on the doorsill, and a uniformed man entered, giving Brad time recite the product description in his head. "Mrs. Rogers? Your water heaters are ready to use," the man said.

"Wonderful," she said. "Help yourself to cognac, Harrison."

"Thank you, ma'am." Harrison pushed through the screen, along with two other men whose excitement seemed to grow as they neared the bottle on the table back in the parlor.

Her magnanimity had always impressed Brad, especially coming from a woman who despised religion. She had riches undreamed of, yet let workmen pass in and out like so many mosquitoes. Of course they would have been checked out.

"Tricky mercury scatters after every micro-meteorite hit, then settles back into the hole thus created," he explained. "Filling holes obviously diminishes its surface coverage, but that's where our bio-engineering pays off. Tricky mercury has a bionic-genetic aspect that allows it to replicate, like a living cell, and replace the outer layers of varnish. It would be, in effect, a sort of eternal protection layer for the Sign's outer surface."

Marilyn beamed. "Well, now, what part of the Sign would get the first application? Let's have a look. Don't forget your wine."

The sun blazed well below the arc of the Sign now, setting into the mountains, and the taste of autumn again threatened to paste Francine's face on one of the shapely bodies down on the walks, or squeeze the smell of her perfume up and into the air. Brad leaned against the window and held his breath. *I'm doing this for you, Francine, for that rich faith you felt, even though I never could.*

It was what he told himself in moments of doubt. He ordered his thoughts to be quiet.

Marilyn belched. "Just how much will a complete application cost an old broad like me?"

"How much do you have?" His standard smart-ass reply, and she laughed. How much is there in the treasury of all the planets in the solar system, he could have asked. How much cash does God carry in the pocket of his jeans?

Before answering seriously, Brad studied the monstrosity once more. A towering three-dimensional placard visible and readable from every inhabited planet in the Solar System. Himmel Gesellschaft's incredible magnetic optics project of fifty years ago used synchronized magnification screens to defy the vast distances of space, making the glyphs on the sign readable from the military outpost on Mercury all the way to Jupiter's four moon colonies. Thus, the Sign dominated the nighttime sky wherever humans dwelled. No old man, nor young child could escape its ominous arch, its depressing message.

He swallowed and gave her the real answer. "About seventy quadrillion dollars." Mrs. Rogers didn't flinch.

"My, my. That puts your commission at about a trillion-two. That'll start the girls in the singles bars flocking around again, eh?"

He wiggled his eyebrows suggestively. The playboy persona was part of his cover. He broke his vows only when he knew spies were watching. As a priest, Francine has been his only true transgression. Suddenly, the low-angled sunshine dimmed in the shadow of a blast of untold proportions. "Crap, that's going to be huge," he said.

He closed his eyes, squinting just enough to watch her, but as the first ruffles of the shockwave moved through the atmosphere, a commotion turned him around.

Harrison and his workmen were laughing, pushing one another around the parlor like schoolkids. Marilyn waved. "Oh, go ahead, boys. Finish the bottle if you wish."

They answered with a spontaneous cheer at the same moment the building began to roll and buck. Shoppers froze in place on the parking lot, glancing up at the gray-brown cloud billowing around the just-awakened evening star. The Sign looked the same as ever.

"Idiots," Marilyn whispered. She quitted the window to straighten the doilies on the end tables.

Brad sipped his wine, praying it would give him the Great Lady's calm. Stick to the plan, he told himself. He would use the weapon on the next visit, if he saw fit. Or he might just tell the Council to stuff themselves.

He could hear the carping Church spies in the break room, each touting a different strategy of how to finally make the immortal Mrs. Rogers *bleed*. If they were so smart, why weren't they here?

Marilyn hummed, and Harrison's boys chuckled and sputtered, no doubt sharing the latest dirty jokes. Brad read the parsec-sized picto-glyphs on the Sign for the thousandth time. He was one of few living to whom the metallurgists had revealed their art – the way the symbols were designed, then attached with iridium shafts in titanium sheaths whose neutrons reacted in the cold vacuum of space until they became one with the magnetic neutrino bed that provided the backbone of the vast arch. The tale the symbols told was so damning that it had stifled Church membership for an era, reducing the Universal Faith to little more than a cabinet-level position.

In glacier-like animation, the pictures told how Marilyn Rogers parlayed her husband's inheritance into a fortune through shrewd business and development deals. Then she won the Galactic Lottery. Rigged the machine, it was rumored. Then the tour of the Great Casinos – the bitch was psychic, they said. She doubled, then tripled her winnings, broke the Bank of Mars, until her fortune was so great that she eventually owned eleven of the twelve inhabitable planets and moons outright.

Then came the glyph of her son falling ill, and slipping into a coma. There was the courageous doctor who revived him for a time, holding aloft his beaker of miracle drugs. But the picture of the son falling back onto his pillows was bigger.

Enter the Priest, Father Lewis. There, in high-relief acid titanium, was the figure of the younger Mrs. Rogers, kissing his ring, following the good preacher back to his quarters, stripping off her clothes and tempting him.

"Embarrassing, but true." Marilyn's voice startled him. Her psychic abilities ebbed and flowed, and only his supreme discipline could keep her away from the wrong thoughts. Brad kept reading: Father Lewis did not yield, and the pictures took on a new tone: Mrs. Rogers followed the holy man's tutelage and converted. Soon after she joined, the Church grew rich beyond imagination. But Cameron slipped deeper toward death in spite of her prayers.

Father Lewis introduced her to the Six Apostles of the Modern Era. For a price, they promised her son would live, and if he died, he would at least be admitted into Heaven. The saga continued past the peak of the sign's arc, into the sad black script of how Cameron Rogers finally succumbed, then the horrible frieze that showed – in stick figures, some moving, some frozen in place – how the soul of Cameron was turned away at the Pearly Gates, and condemned to Hell for eternity.

Father Lewis and the Apostles took pity on the grieving mother, and promised the boy a second judgment if she only paid more. Marilyn's incredible fortune was halved, the high-flying pictures demonstrated, but Cameron's spirit never emerged from the Pit. Here, the chronicle grew frightening, and even dumb school-less children could understand its stark message: Why join the Great Church? They couldn't save Marilyn's son, thus they can't save anyone. Brad felt Marilyn's gaze boring into him.

"My darling," she said. "That is why I have done business with you for so long. You truly feel my pain."

"Yes, Ma'am."

She stared into her glass, possessed of a sudden, strange mood, it seemed. Harrison's men were arguing now, gesturing at each other with fists. Shouldn't they be dismissed?

"Marry me, Brad." She said the words quietly.

His mouthful of wine came spewing out. Thankfully, he was able to aim out the window. "What?"

"Marry me. When I die, the fortune can belong to you, instead of that hot alien feline."

"Marilyn, I don't--" Brad sputtered like an imbecile, but recovered. "My dear, you'll never die, so why worry?"

"Shut up, Brad. You know what I'm talking about. They keep washing the records, so you can't know I'm almost three hundred now. Don't worry, all the parts still work. They should, I've paid for new ones twice over. But the day is coming. Look at that." She gestured toward the arch, glowing brighter now in the gathering darkness. "You can have it. Plus the secret formulas. You'll outlive me by fifty years at least, and have all the women you want. Women of every stripe and race and number of appendages."

"Who's washing what records--"

Her raised hand stopped any protest, and she leaned close, closer than she had ever been, and whispered directly into his ear. "The formulas. The secret metallurgy recipes you've been trying to get from me for the last five years."

He backed away. "What do you mean? I haven't-"

"Oh, yes you have, Priest."

The accusation was sharp, final, driven home by the cold sparkle in her eyes. His stomach fell away. Of course she would know, had probably always known. Money buys everything, including Holy Brothers. He vowed silently to find the stool pigeon and expose him. Unless she had other plans this night.

"Don't take it so personally," she said, licking her ancient lips. "I still love you, and when you have the money and the power, you will see the light."

"I'm a former technician with the Titanium Rangers," his cover story started spilling out on its own. "My wife died ten years ago, so I'm a widower–"

"Spare me, Brad-y Boy. You are a member of the Buddhist-Jesuit Spy Cadre. Yes, there was a Francine, but that's because you broke your vows – what, a hundred times with her? So you're a sinner, like the rest of us. You're the enemy, Brad. But I love you for your faith. And lack of it. For your play acting, as it were." She laughed, and patted his cheek.

"Marilyn, you're talking crazy--"

"Enough with the lies, Brad. No more of those. I'm going to die. After that, you may do with the secret formulas what you will."

Close again. "This is a serious offer, young man. If you have any doubts, you should know that I've paid for certain delightful sexual positions unknown since the start of the Space Travel Era. They can be yours, too."

She kissed him voraciously, a kiss that might never have ended, because the devils that lie in wait in the mind of any man were coming out of the woodwork.

In a swift moment, the fantasies were back, washing over him. Becoming the boy-toy of the wealthy Dame, the living goddess from another era, the lady of leisure, the vacations and cover stories of wild parties that would have turned Gomorrah blue, not to mention the legion of demure sycophant debutantes that made up the ancient woman's posse.

The kiss continued – Her lips must belong to the Dark One, the way they pressed in on his. Her playful tongue penetrated, conjuring voices in his head, all enticing him – they seemed to mimic his own voice, down to his own laughter as it would be heard at the raging revelries and blow-out orgies that could be his new life, if only he said, "yes."

He was caught, as surely as Francine's precious mouth had captured him, and he pressed his lips back in response – meeting magic with strength – harder, slowing the visions down, admitting the more salacious scenes in dribs and drabs. He could have lived in that kiss for eternity, but a loud noise pulled them apart. He fell back against the wall, groggy.

"Bradley. Help." Her voice suddenly old, squeaky. He looked up. Harrison and his cohorts were not drunk at all, but crowded into the doorway, all three leveling blast rods at the Woman of the Sign.

It happened too fast – Harrison's speech, "Marilyn Rogers, we execute you in the name of the Brabant-Six Colony on Mars, whose children have been denied Holy Communion because of you –"

"Traitors," Marilyn cried. For an instant Brad froze, but a flash of orange turned his head – not a blast from the rods, but the Firecat. The creature did a rapid pirouette by the bookshelf, stood on its hind legs, raised its front paws, and emitted the scariest screaming, moaning, crackling whine Brad had ever heard.

"*Eeehhhhhh--*" The sound elevated to a deafening whistle.

"Damned devil--" Harrison started to say. His eyes blinked wildly, and his thugs recoiled against the parlor cornice, but it was as if Brad's body knew what to do. So easy if he just let them kill her and be done, but the Prelate had claimed her Judgment for the Church alone. The shell was out of Brad's pocket before the assassins could regain their stances.

Click. Click. Click. One trigger-pull for each target. "Shoot and duck," the science advisors had insisted. "Get in the way, and her punishment will be yours." Not knowing what to expect, Brad leaped across the window and forced Marilyn down, covering her with his own body.

From the floor, Brad saw Harrison's assassins buckle, as if hit by invisible projectiles. Their feet left the floor in unison, yet the men were still alive, rising into the air, dumbfounded, pained looks across their faces.

Gazing down from his hovering perch in mid-air, near the ceiling, Harrison's eyes met Brad's. Lips moved. The foreman was trying to say something. But before he could get it out, the three floating men were propelled, tumbling, out the window just above Brad's head.

Stunned, he watched, and cried out to no one, "What does it do?" The shell still vibrated in his hand, but his gaze was riveted on the three bodies flying through space, up toward the waking stars, and a deafening sound of glass breaking echoed through the atmosphere.

The writhing, twisting, airborne forms that used to be assassins seemed to change in nature after that, and sailed directly for the Sign. All three workmen flattened out and grew to enormous proportions, like two-dimensional sailing kites, humongous cartoons of themselves, until they were pasted, as if by some great unseen hand, onto a blank space in the lower side of the great arch.

"What in the name of the Holy God?"

Harrison and his workers were unworldly giants now, and part of the Sign, frozen into poses of aiming their blast rods. The attempted assassination of Marilyn Rogers was suddenly posted for all to see, a visual that told the latest episode of the Lady's tumultuous life – the would-be killers had become picto-glyphs on the largest edifice in the Firmament.

Marilyn hovered by his shoulder now, gazing upwards, disheveled, but only for a moment. Then the ancient dame adjusted her shawl and nodded toward the buzzing shell in Brad's hand. "Well, Priest? Are you finished with your shooting? Or will there be more?"

With shaking hands, he laid the shell on the short bookshelf nearby. What did they send him here to do? Those soulless Priests wanted Marilyn tacked up onto her own sign for as long as it stood. Eternity, in other words. A simple click would transform her from a flesh-and-blood child of God into a cartoon prisoner of the structure she had labored all of her life to build. He gaped in horror at Harrison and his henchmen, those would-be heroes who now suffered a fate worse than Hell itself. No wonder the shell couldn't be demonstrated. They had tricked a priest into wielding a tool of the Devil.

"No. No more," he said, breathing hard. He met her gaze. "The Sign. It's not about your son's rejection from Heaven at all, is it? You built that Sign as a chronicle of your own life. The Sign is the story of your vanity, Marilyn Rogers."

She stared with hard eyes. "Of course the Sign is my story, you whelp. One that will never end." Her fingers gripped his bicep. Then the other hand, and her limbs wrapped around his torso in an embrace too strong for a woman of two – or three centuries.

"No," he said.

"Yes, my love. The Sign can be your story, too. You have but to decide to sin again." With deft movements she unbuckled his belt, and his pants fell to his knees.

"No." This cry was louder, but it did not stop her groping hands. "I can't sin again, Marilyn," he begged. "The first time was too painful – Wait!"

Her hands were already under his shirt, searching, but she paused – maybe psychic enough to feel his shock – Brad froze in place, staring at the shell. The Firecat had removed it from the bookcase, and sat in the middle of the floor, with the weapon turned so that the manifold pointed straight at them.

"No." Brad screamed, but the creature did not flinch. Brad thought to lunge, but not quickly enough.

Click. Click.

The next sound he heard was that of breaking glass – the cells of his body were the glass, and Marilyn still hugged him close, her aged features becoming crystalline before his very eyes. The bright stores of the shopping center fell away beneath them, as did bustling nighttime cities, then worlds.

He could not feel the flattening out, the growth in size, could only guess that those things were happening. Perhaps all things were relative. But he did feel his back slam against a solid wall. The world blinked. Then flashed on again, the whole curve of the Earth ablaze with twinkling lights below him.

Something was quiet – too, too quiet – he realized the throb of blood in his ears was no more, his feelings evaporating into wisps, and with them, emotions.

He did feel the distinct suction of becoming one with something that tasted of steel and oil and titanium. An iron, acrid flavor invaded his very skin, oozed through his being. He could no longer see Marilyn, could only feel her there at his side, one stiff, solid hand up his shirt, the other frozen in the act of caressing his petrified buttocks. A thought – a silly, terrifying thought passed through his mind, like a feather on the wind: her hands, already losing their warmth, would stay where they were, cemented for eternity, just as his pants would remain forever crumpled down around his ankles. Both he and the old lady had become part of the invulnerable frieze, the eternal story of the Sign.

He expected pain, but felt only the last wisp of stomach acid rising through his mouth, a mouth he could not close – would it be sculptured open in surprise forever? He knew he should make peace with God in the instant he had left, but his mind was invaded by images of the smart-assed Priests peering at the sign from their break room and chortling about "the last temptation of Friar Bradley."

The lights of the cities far below started to dim. Happy lights fading into a sick, hollow envy, an envy borne of the laughter, the toasts of the revelers down there in those malls, the chattering of shoppers and theater crowds, the growls of gluttonous satisfaction, the moans of lovers in their beds and all those Heavenly sounds that belonged beneath those lights, sounds he would never hear again from this frozen slab a million miles above everything.

A tear settled and froze on Brad's flat metallic cheek – he could smell – no, taste it: tricky mercury. The bitch had already made a deal with a rival firm –

To hell with business! And with Faith! He felt his brain cells shutting down, sharp pains as they burst in droves, but he would not die with a prayer. He wanted his last conscious thought to be of that day with Francine in the park – yes, Francine. In the park—

Instead, in his last surge of evaporating, carbonated blood, a vision of Twinky the Firecat appeared before him, almost as if the beast had been telepathically squatting in the closets of his mind until the right instant to send him a farewell message.

The vision flashed, crystal clear: In it, Twinky slinked through the warm glow of those Earthly lights, buying rounds of drinks, sleeping with every woman who had a feline fetish and a prodigious sexual appetite. An interloper with fur and a sensuous orange tail, drunk and high and sated and popular and protected and coveted by all as he squandered the greatest fortune in the history of the cosmos.

A fortune that could have been Brad's.

THE END

The Termite Queen
By Bull Marquette

The first time Dell Shaw saw her was from the patio of the duplex condo he was trying to buy. She came clumping across the deserted beach that lined Lido Bay, past the village of six-figure double-wides, then the two-story beach houses that had to be seven-figures, maybe more. There was something wrong with her shoes, and instead of a bikini, she clutched some huge coat around her stumbling form. A cloud moved, allowing the low sun to hit her so that he could finally see clearly that it was a full-length mink and that her wobbly high heels were drilling large clam flutes in the sand, then popping out only with effort. She was breathing hard.

"I'm sorry to keep you waiting, Mr. Shaw," Arlene Remington's voice came from inside the screen doors. "I know I have that promissory form here somewhere."

"Not a problem," Dell said. But it was. His glass of soda was already empty, and there might be other bidders, and the taxes he would have to pay on his 401k distribution would haunt him for the rest of his life. There were a million reasons, signs, even, that he should just call it quits, go back to the car and drive away. But he thought of Lizzie, and didn't.

Besides, the blond, short-haired goddess plodding toward him was just another colorful facet of life in this mysterious paradise of overpriced real estate and lapping waves. This was where he belonged. Home – Lizzy would have called it that, and he had promised her.

The goddess was now almost to the short wall across the narrow cul-de-sac that served as a boat launch. Children's laughter lilted from a passing Duffy boat. Two kayakers skidded toward the smooth beach, halfway down, and across the water, boats in the marina were festooned with flags. Behind them, even larger mansions over on Lido Isle glowed in the slanted sun rays, some flying flags themselves. Those might start at ten million, for all Dell could guess.

"I found it," Mrs. Remington called out. More shuffling. In another ten minutes, Dell would stake his claim to this corner of paradise.

The goddess sat and on the wall and swung her legs over, a short distance away from the man who had been reading a newspaper since Dell's arrival. The man didn't look up, and she crossed Dell's view of the serene Bay.

"Hi," Dell said. "Must be tough in the sand with those shoes."

Still moving, she turned her head and squinted. "I like your shirt," she said, in the husky, soft voice that God gives some blondes. "It's happy." She reached the sidewalk and opened the gate of the dingy three-story building next door, and clopped up the outside staircase without greeting the two workmen who were descending, laden with debris. They hung their heavy garbage bags over the rail so she could pass.

"Thanks," Dell said, too late. He was already embarrassed that he had worn the blue-and-yellow shirt with the red parrots. Paradise fever had gripped him all week.

The sliding door opened effortlessly, another mark of the neighborhood he was in, and Arlene Remington emerged, sheaf of documents under one arm, cup of coffee in the opposite hand. "Here we are." She arranged the papers into two stacks.

"Does she live there?" Dell asked.

"Who?" When Arlene turned, only the two dust-covered men remained on the stairs. "They're remodeling," she said. "Tearing out the walls. Damn thing's full of asbestos." She gestured toward the man across the street, who was now marking on the newspaper with a pen. "That's the owner, George Nakamichi. Oh, don't worry, there's not a shred of asbestos in this place."

"I'm sure," Dell said. The way dust was flying next door, the goddess's home seemed beyond repair. He wondered if she were Nakamichi's wife, or just a tenant.

"OK," Mrs. Remington began. "My only concern is that my lawyer is all over me about selling this without a realtor. I really don't want to spend the rest of my life in lawsuits with you. We're about the same age – you're retiring here?"

"Yes. I teach English at Pepperdine. This is my last semester."

"Early retirement? Hell, I'm sixty-two, and you -- you're--"

"Fifty-nine-and-a-half," Dell said with a chuckle. "Two months beyond the penalty age for my 401k."

Her royal-bitch air softened the least bit, and she even chuckled with him. "Sinking the whole nest egg, eh? Well, don't worry. You keep the place neat as a pin and advertise on the Internet. I've already told Charlie – he's my computer guy – about you. He'll keep the website up for peanuts. As I told you, you can get three-thousand clams a week for the upstairs, minimum, during the summer. It's a bad month when you have even a week vacant."

"I'm excited," Dell said, speaking over the rumbling in his gut. He was a teacher, not a businessman, and had lost every one of the few negotiations he had ever entered into. "Well, you don't have to worry about going to court. The house checks out, and you've kept it immaculate." Pointing, he whispered. "Not like next door."

"Don't worry about that," she said. "George is putting a bundle into fixing it. Poor bastard, they made him move out until it's done. He's going to live on the second floor. He rents out the two units downstairs, and now he'll have the third floor usable, too. That will command a penthouse price, believe me. Put a balcony up there and you can see across the peninsula to the Pacific."

"Beautiful," Dell said, and took a deep breath. The card had to be played. "Speaking of lawyers, I think they're a pain in the ass, too. But mine looked at all the comps in this neighborhood. He recommends that I not pay over two million-three."

"What?" Arlene swelled and stood, knocking her rattan chair over in the process. A sudden breeze caught the folds of her flowered caftan and made the chimes ring. "Who the hell said you could have a two-hundred thousand dollar discount?"

Dell's teeth closed down onto his tongue. Stay the course that Bill laid out, he told himself, praying. "Mrs. Remington, the appraisal was for two million-three."

"Screw the appraisers," she said. She paced only for a second, then loomed over him. "I said three thousand a week, minimum. I can usually get four in August. Twenty-five hundred in the winter. The people from Denver and New York flock here to get out of the snow. Damn you, you can rent a trailer over there and let out both floors."

She paced, heaving her bulk around the patio at random. Dell's fingers closed around the empty glass. "Mrs. Remington, this is just business. No insult intended. It's a beautiful home."

"Well, then show a little respect." She waved a finger. "Stay right there. I'm going to have to talk to Spiegel about this."

She moved inside like a storm cloud. Dell's mouth was dry, and he was thankful that the sun chose that moment to go back into hiding. Damn it all, why not go ahead and pay full-boat? The fog was here almost every day, they said. Lizzy would have grown tired of it, but he loved the cool. In one of the back bedrooms, Arlene's voice sounded frantic, and Dell took the chance to swing

over the patio wall the same way the goddess had. He
wanted to drink in the still, sweet bay again.

The two workmen rattled in Spanish. One of them
was named Carlos, apparently. Dell nodded to them.
They responded with smiles, then resumed tossing their
bags of asbestos into the blue, truck-sized dumpster-for-
hire. A small boat pulled into the dock, its pilot tossing
fishing gear out onto the wood planks. Dell could buy a
boat, too, if she only met his price.

"Having trouble with the old biddy?" the man
with the newspaper said. Dell stepped toward him. Not a
newspaper – it was a racing form.

Dell introduced himself. "You play the horses?"

"Hell, it's all I can do." Nakamichi threw a thumb
over his shoulder. "I'm going broke with this damned
remediation."

"Oh?"

"The inspectors want this. They want that. Then
the city council passes some tax law to get around Prop
Thirteen, and I don't have enough cash to fight them.
Now it's termites."

"Termites?" Dell studied the building. Rusted
metal windows, peeling paint. One of the doorways
downstairs looked neat and new, but he guessed the
tenant had done that himself.

"Yes, goddam it. I'm going to have to kick
Brendan out while we tent the whole thing. Don't worry,
I don't think they've spread to any other buildings. Old
Arlene checks for that sort of thing every two weeks,
seems like."

"Brendan? Is that her name?" Dell asked, peering for a glimpse of her in the upper windows.

"Huh?" The racing form sagged. "Brendan's my tenant. He's got a dog named Flossy. Lives half the time here and half on his boat out there. My other renter moved out when Jabba the Hutt started all this crap."

"Jabba the Hutt? Like in Star Wars?"

Nakamichi laughed and sneered at the same time. "That's what I call the government. The system. They prey on the rich. Welfare cases come down here and surf. We pay for them to surf and drink beer. The rest of us are drones, breaking our humps to feed the Termite Queen. That was the inspiration for Jabba the Hutt, you know. A termite queen is just a big blob that all the workers have to feed."

"Yeah, I guess so." Dell let himself chuckle. He had never thought of himself as rich, but here he was, about to shell out two-million dollars, the fruit of thirty-five years of "hump-busting" for himself, with the bulk of Lizzy's retirement fund thrown in, to boot.

Still, this guy was a loudmouth, so Dell decided to put up at least a little defense. "But with all the taxes you're paying, how do you have money to play the horses?"

A serious, maybe even sad look. "Sometimes, you have to gamble to realize your dreams," Nakamichi said.

Back on the patio, Arlene slammed the sliding screen open, cell phone in hand. "Hey." A wave. "Just hang on another five minutes." She disappeared back into the condo's shadows.

Dell had a sudden inspiration, and caught Nakamichi's eye. "Can I go up and look?"

A shrug. "Sure. Just be careful, and don't breathe that shit. I don't want you to sue me for lung cancer."

"I promise I won't."

"Hey." Nakamichi pointed at the form. "What do you think about this one – Paradise Lost? It's a filly."

"Good name, but a little worrisome, too." The landlord nodded and Dell retraced the steps the goddess had taken through the gate and up the outside staircase.

The second floor was a hollowed-out shell, and Carlos and his subordinate were arguing about the placement of a sheet of wood paneling. They stopped when they saw Dell.

"No, Senor. Sorry." Carlos pinched his nose. "Asbestos. Against the law for you to be here." His colleague wore a blue mask, but Carlos didn't.

"Sorry. Can I just look for a minute? I have Mr. Nakamichi's permission."

Carlos licked his lips. "OK, but don't walk in *la cocina*. Flooring will be here tomorrow."

"Sure."

There wasn't much to see here. An ancient refrigerator, rust-marked sink, pieces of ripped carpet and a bathroom so rude that it made Dell wonder what tourists would pay to rent this place. He went up the stairs to the third floor. Here, the rooms still had doors.

Did she come up this far? Dell moved, though he suddenly knew he shouldn't be here. There might be other tenants – but all the doors were open, and when he looked through the third one, he saw her, bending down over an old-fashioned cabinet hi-fi. The room was a shambles of boxes and broken furniture. The only mattress stood propped up on the wall, and her mink lay crumpled in a pile. But he didn't look long at those things. She rose up and stared at him. She was naked.

"I'm sorry," Dell managed to sputter. "I – Mr. Nakamichi said I could come up."

She might have been thirty. Or twenty or forty. The perfect body to go with the voice at any age. Still wearing the high heels, she reached casually for the mink, not to put it on, but simply to hold in front of herself, though a maddening amount of her body remained on display. He should have quit the door already, because he shouldn't be here. But she looked into his eyes again.

"Are you Mrs. Nakamichi?" he asked, breathless.

No response to the question. Not even a flutter. "They're making me move out. Putting a tent over the place," she said.

"Oh? Then you rent from him?"

She didn't answer, but stayed focused on her plight. Her soft words caressed, even as they asked for help. "He spent ten thousand dollars for Flossy's hip replacement. But he's spending even more to get rid of me." A hopeless voice. Eyes full of pained rejection.

"Flossy?" Dell asked, trying to understand. "Isn't that the name of the guy's dog downstairs?"

"Yes. They replaced her hip. I've got pictures of her x-ray on my cell phone. Do you want to see?" When she moved, so did the mink, revealing first one breast, then another. She had to be in her early thirties, he decided. Then again, Dell felt he was talking to a child.

"No, that's OK. Where will you move while they dust the termites?"

She shrugged, and shook her head. "Don't you think he should treat everyone who lives here the same? I mean, after ten thousand dollars, I thought he was out of money. But he found some more." A tear came, and she looked down to caress the floor-length coat. "I had to move out from next door the same way."

Dell pointed toward his own condo-to-be. "You mean there?"

Another head-shake. "No. The other way. Did I tell you I like your parrots? You seem like someone who-_"

But her voice trailed off, and the force holding Dell in place finally let go. "I'll let you get dressed," he said. "Sorry for the intrusion." She couldn't possibly live in this wreck of a room, could she? But he didn't have the nerve to ask. "I'm moving in next door, next month. Maybe. I hope I'll see you again."

"If I'm here." She looked down again, and waved a hand, dismissing him in a gesture reminiscent of a queen ordering a knight on an errand. Dell staggered downstairs, feeling like a balloon had been blown up inside his heart.

On the street, Nakamichi was conferring with Mrs. Remington. He looked over wryly. "Arlene tells me you're some big professor."

"Pepperdine," Dell said.

"Why can't you academic types teach the politicians anything?" A finger shot forward. "You may have it figured out, how you can afford this place, but I'm telling you the big fat termite queen will bleed you dry. Sometimes, I think the government goes around, planting the damn things in houses. You'll need twice the asking price, Pal. Just you wait and see."

Arlene slapped at his arm. "Shut your mouth, George, or I'll come spoiling the next deal you try to make." She turned on Dell with what passed for a smile. "Come over here. We gotta talk." Dell's heart beat. She did say the word *deal*.

Nakamichi started to retreat, but a pickup with white-and-blue Newport Beach markings entered the dead end, yellow lights flashing. "Oh, God, the city inspectors again," he said, rolling his eyes at Dell, gesturing toward the new arrivals. "If you're a liberal, Prof, better enjoy it now. You won't be for long."

"Don't listen to him," Arlene said. "George, you boys keep it down, or I'll have to conduct business inside, and I don't want to turn on a fan." She sat down first.

"There's good news and bad news, Mr. Shaw."

"Yes?"

"My attorney, Jeremy Spiegel advises me to accept your offer. That's the good news. I know you're pinching pennies and I don't mind being outmaneuvered, but I need money, too. You'll soon find out that most of the citizens of the peninsula and the islands are house poor."

Sweat eased down Dell's temples, but he resisted the urge to wipe it. "Meaning what, Mrs. Remington? Are you going to make a counter offer?"

She gestured toward the second floor. "See that? I haven't been able to rent for a week, because Spiegel is afraid some vacationer might stub his toe, sue, and hang up my sale for a year." Dell's gaze fell to the stack of papers where she rested her hands. The topmost form was titled "Termite Inspection." At the bottom, stamps and checkmarks.

She leaned closer. "If I sell to you this minute, it'll be another four or five weeks before we close. Multiply that by three grand. That's money I'll be missing out on, money I damn well need. Figure it out yourself."

"You want me to add fifteen thousand to my offer?" Dell felt himself wince. Roger was Lizzy's brother, a built-in attorney ever since the wedding, and he said only a dumb shit would go above an appraisal.

Arlene blinked. "Go over to the dock and think it over. I'll be here," she said.

He rose, but had to ask. "Do you know the name of Mr. Nakamichi's tenant upstairs?"

"He lives alone."

"No, I mean up on the third floor."

She huffed. "I already told you, he's fixing it up so he can rent it. I've lived with that eyesore for years."

"That's not what I'm asking." Dell let his frustration spill over. "I mean, does he have a wife? Or a mistress? Who's that blonde up there?"

"George has a mistress?" She guffawed, then silenced herself. Nakamichi and the city guys had moved over onto the sand. Their discussion looked heated. "I'm afraid you've got the wrong idea about George." She punctuated the revelation with a wink.

"Give me five minutes."

He was over the short wall and out on the dock in only twenty steps or so. Wasn't this exactly what he wanted? Not just near the beach, but on it? The fisherman's boat was gone, and two cabin cruisers plowed by, their drivers waving beers at each other. A movement made Dell turn his head. The goddess was standing by a stanchion on the lower part of the dock. Clothed now. Cutoffs, a halter top, cell phone clipped to her belt.

She turned and beckoned, as if she already knew he was there. "Come look," she said. He stood next to her. She had showered somewhere, or sprayed perfume– a sweet smell of gardenias, or some flowering tree. "See?"

In the long shadows just below the surface of the water, a school of jellyfish undulated in easy view. Gossamer white, with strange forms under their flowing dresses and four bright-white membranes arranged symmetrically on their top canopies. The goddess gripped his arm without warning, making his heart beat faster. "Aren't they beautiful?"

"Yes. I've never seen anything – like this. I mean, like them."

"See those bright circles that make a diamond shape?"

"Yes."

"My mother taught me that they give those to the sand dollars when they die."

There was a strange truth to it, for the shapes looked exactly like tiny, translucent drawings of sand dollars. Dell felt himself react, and was sorry, for her hand fell. "What a charming story," he said, scrambling to stay in her good graces. "Do sand dollars have those same four markings? I don't remember--"

"Not four, silly. They give them one each. Each jellyfish can give to four sand dollars, see?" She looked up now, and gave him one of those smiles that force you to smile back. She didn't seem like college material. Did it matter?

Dell pointed down the long row of docks that stuck out from the large houses. "So you're saying you lived in that tan one there before you moved here to the corner?"

"Yes." She turned, and actually put one arm around his waist while she pointed with the other. "I lived there a year. And before that, the beige one next to it, for six months. Before that, the duplex with the green awning. They let me stay there a long time." The slightest hug, the dreamiest, begging stare. Dell wanted to speak, but what interesting thing could he push past his heart – which was now stuck in his throat. "So can you understand why I hate leaving here? Where else can I watch jellyfish and play with Flossie?" She finished with a soft, magical squeeze of his hand.

"It's terrible that you have to leave," he sputtered. "But Mr. Nakamichi's right over there. Surely he'll give you a lease, after the work's finished. Come with me. I'd like to talk to both of you." This was the chance to solve the puzzle, Dell thought. Either Nakamichi had a claim on her, or he didn't. But she disengaged, and started down the wooden ramp between docks.

"Sorry. My friends brought me some food."

She crossed, and leaped skillfully to the next dock, and something inside him fell. In an instant, she was yards away, entering the lengthening shadows. But when she reached the sidewalk, she stopped, turned, and blew him a kiss.

He watched her disappear into an alley between the houses, then looked up to see one of those red-orange sunset celebrations that he and Lizzy always worshipped. The sun must be hitting the ocean. In the clouds above, he could almost see Lizzy as she lay dying, could see himself making her two promises: one, that he would move to the ocean, the other that he would begin again.

Of course the last one was a lie, because no one had ever been like her or could ever be like her. He stopped, so dizzy that he had to grab onto the asbestos dumpster for support. What was happening to him?

The city truck was gone, and Nakamichi barked orders to the construction boys at the other end of the long dumpster, as if they didn't know how to padlock the thing. From here, Dell could see Arlene drumming her fingers on the patio table, but he paused just once more.

"Mr. Nakamichi, I've been trying to ask you. Who is that woman that lives in your building? The pretty one?"

The landlord scowled, playing dumb, perhaps. But Carlos looked up with a jerk. "I got one tenant, I told you," Nakamichi said. "And he's got a dog. Now don't tell me you're a liberal and seeing ghosts to boot."

"No. Sorry. I hope we'll be friends as well as neighbors," Dell said, watching as Carlos hustled his *compadre* into the garage.

"Hey, Prof, I meant what I said about feeding Jabba the Hut. A fool and his money are soon parted."

"Yeah." Dell moved away, threw one leg over the patio wall and took a deep breath.

"I'll take it," he said as he sat down.

Arlene's eyes narrowed in the failing light. "You'll take what?" she asked.

"The five weeks. You accept my offer of two-three, and I'll pay you five weeks' rent. I know someone who needs a place to stay."

Even in the dimness, a broad smile. "Well, now we're getting somewhere," she said. She rose, switched on the patio light, and they signed the papers.

When Dell stepped back onto the street, Nakamichi was just driving away, cell phone to his ear. Placing bets on tomorrow's horses? But there was another truck in the cul-de-sac, an old one. The workmen were climbing into it. Dell moved quickly enough to grab the driver's door before Carlos could close it.

"Tell me," Dell demanded.

"*Que*? Tell you what?"

"About the woman. Do you know her? You know something."

Carlos's mouth worked, and he met the gaze of the other one before he spoke. "She brings the termites. Andre and me, we work this part of town for years. First she comes, then the termites." A shrug. "Maybe it's better than asbestos, but the rich people's houses are still destroyed. *Buenos noches*."

Dell let go of the handle, and they drove away. He walked swiftly toward Newport Boulevard, and found the meter flashing and a citation stuck in his car's windshield wipers.

He pulled coins out of his pocket automatically, wondering whether to stick them into the meter, or just drive home. They shone softly in the dusk, glistening like the circles on the jellyfish. How much time would it take to track the goddess down and tell her the good news? An inner voice answered – she would find him. He inserted two coins into the meter, and turned back toward the bay. Sometimes, you have to gamble to realize your dreams.

THE END

An Agent for Mama Bear
By Bull Marquette

I had written six novels, none of them published. I write books about being psychic, because I am, partly. Like a ball player who gets his share of hits, but only blasts one home run per year, I could only be described as a minor-leaguer in the ESP game.

So it wasn't often that I expected to be visited by a Grand Slam, a really big message from my Sixth Sense, but on a crisp September morning as I climbed into my aging Chevy van, there it was. Like a vision hovering before me, or a disembodied voice whispering in my ear, a profound message came from the ether: After ten years of submitting my novels to agents for representation and being rejected thousands of times, today, the first day of the Mountain Home Writers Conference, my luck was about to change.

I was almost too titillated to drive to the airport. Of course it would happen now. There were five agents coming in from New York, all on the same plane, and

Mrs. Sotheby, the conference organizer, had enlisted me to pick them up. She even discounted my conference registration fee for making the long, difficult drive deep into the mountains, up winding roads all the way to the six thousand foot level and the Eagle's Rest, the luxury hotel that hosted the annual confab.

"It's a rare opportunity, Charlie," Mrs. Sotheby said. "Five agents as a captive audience. But don't pitch your novel to all of them at once. Play it cool. Show them you're a regular fella. Get to know them, and pick the best ones to try to convince to represent your novel to publishers during the next two days of the conference. You know how important a literary agent is to your career, and you know how to deal with them. You're a shoo-in."

The van fairly floated through the airport security checkpoint and into short-term parking. An unpublished novelist chauffeuring agents was like a village idiot taxiing members of the Royal family. Worse – this village idiot was about to pack a bunch of persnickety New Yorkers into a jalopy with a sagging headliner. But it had a new engine and plenty of seats, and my burst of precognition wrapped around me like protective chain mail. Today my pumpkin was a golden carriage, my success already written in the stars.

While I stowed leather suitcases by Papworth and Coach in the cargo hold, the psychic forces dropped a clarification into my brain: There were other agents scheduled to speak, but it would be one of these five – three women and two men – who stood, blinking against the California sun, who would sign me.

Of course I hoped it would be Sy Nanderjack. His penchant for representing best-sellers was legendary even before the Germans took over the industry. So powerful, he had even rejected Stephen King after *Pet Sematary*. But any of the others would suffice: Nancy Germain, master of all genres; Dick Rippington, the English cad who kept the ladies laughing with his impatience for the cocktail hour; Janet Stallings, the tiny prim thing whose smile could melt the ice in a highball – I had proof, because when I first met her at a conference in 1998, and my scotch and soda practically boiled over in my hand. Even Brunhilde Marchant, the Bette Midler look-alike, had the moxie I was looking for in an agent. She might land the biggest advance of all.

Sy seemed pleased when I put him in the front passenger seat. The women united in polite tolerance, leaving only Dick to make snide remarks about the foam headliner bits that rained down onto his Brooks Brothers suit.

I drove, playing sophisticated native, lecturing about passing groves of fruit trees, and how grape trays were used to make raisins. I quoted statistics about how many bears were returning to the Sierra after decades on the endangered species list, and generally claimed more mountain knowledge than John Fremont or Jedediah Smith ever possessed. I eased around the curves, to lessen any chances of carsickness. My passengers seemed duly impressed.

I measured them in the rear view mirror, five masters of the publishing universe, their canny countenances framed by headliner stalactites. Which of them would finally recognized my talent and validate this morning's psychic homerun? At the three thousand foot level, Brunhilde threw me a curve.

"I know your scheme, Charlie," she said. "You act like the innocent volunteer, but I received a query from you just yesterday. I'll bet you sent one to every agent in this car."

She was right. You can't judge a book by its cover, but that's exactly how agents decide what books to represent: They read one-page summaries called "queries." Of course, agents don't read them, but delegate that distasteful duty to unpaid interns hot to break into the publishing business. After a decade of submitting, this proof that one of the Elect had actually read one of my peppy synopses brought a smile to my face. But then all hell broke loose. "A history book, isn't it?" she asked.

"History? Nonfiction is good," Sy said, before I could correct Brunhilde. She hadn't read query, only the title, and now everyone in the car had the wrong idea. But I couldn't straighten her out without pitching my novel to all of them at once. Mrs. Sotheby's strategy crumbled like a rock outcropping above the highway.

"Not nonfiction," I said hurriedly. "It's a novel titled *The History of the Universe*. It's an action-thriller with dramatic scenes from the history of everything since the Big Bang. Not just on Earth, but other planets as well." Saying it out loud made it sound a bit convoluted, but I didn't dare admit that.

I didn't have to. Nancy Germain looked skeptical. "Sounds pretty expansive. You need a plot, of course. You know, guy rescues damsel in distress. The usual."

"It's got all that," I insisted. "My expertise is in parapsychology, so when the hero's lover is kidnapped, he uses paranormal abilities to travel all over space and time to rescue her in the grand finale."

On the middle seat, Janet Stallings tugged at her tight dress. "Sounds like it has potential. But do you think you could rewrite it with a little less story?"

I shuddered, and fought to keep the vehicle from plunging into the gorge on the right. Failing Sy, Janet was my ace-in-the-hole. At that conference in Washington years ago, I paid twenty dollars to talk to her for ten minutes. Some hookers don't charge that much, but she was even better looking, and I found her literary knowledge unparalleled.

I downshifted, and my gaze locked with Sy's. "Bread pudding," he said earnestly.

"Huh?"

"That's what's hot now." A fatherly wink. "Do a new recipe book about bread puddings and I can sell it anywhere."

"Duh," Nancy Germain leaned forward, loosing a shower of headliner foam across her forehead. "Who couldn't?"

Sy, this group's obvious alpha male, shrugged. "That presentation at the Tavern pretty well told it all."

"Solid gold, that." Dick Rippington sucked on one of the water bottles I had left in each drink holder. "That little twit's speech will help all of us retire early."

"Speech?" I feigned just enough interest to convince them that I was in the know. If they spilled any powerful industry secrets, someone would have to sign me just to keep me quiet.

"Some muckety-muck seminar we all went to at Tavern on the Green in Central Park," Brunhilde answered, brushing foam bits from her arms. "The talk was called 'Focusing the Market in Unison.' Jeez, is this dandruff?"

In the rear-view mirror, Nancy nodded. "That little psychologist made me think I'd seen the face of God."

"It was a speech on the psychology of literature?" I asked.

"Hell, no. Marketing." Sy scowled. "Watch the TV news guys. This week they all talk about M-S. Next week, lung cancer. A week later, it's spousal abuse. One names a topic, the talk shows pick it up, it becomes a *passion d' jour*. Two months ago everybody in America anguished about ingrown toenails for four days. That's power marketing. It happens when opinion makers act in concert."

I could have quit while I was behind, but curiosity won out. "And that affects the publishing industry how?"

From his perch, snug against Janet's hips, right where I wanted to be, Dick explained. "Ibid, Old Boy. This month, it's Bread Pudding cookbooks. Next fortnight, historicals about the South American conquest. If all publishers push the same topic, we make a market, *capiche*? No more oh, darling-isn't-this-true-literature bollocks. The Germans – they own the publishing industry now, don't you know – simply hate subjectivity."

"We got quarterly numbers to make," Brunhilde cried. "Schmuck agents fifty years ago wasted their lives reading whole manuscripts, looking for diamonds in the rough. This is the age of costume jewelry. Writing is a commodity."

In the back, Nancy sighed. "How else can we compete with MP3s and Game Boys?"

The sun dropped behind the tall trees, dragging my novels with it. How could my precognition this morning – the strongest one ever – be this wrong? I tried another tack. "What about original plots or exciting characters?"

"Bah." Sy dismissed me with a wave. "Ten years from now the only books left will be thriller-memoirs."

"Hear-hear," Dick said. "Average Joe Six-Pack punching up his dull life to make it sound James Bond-ish. Do that, Charlie-boy, and we'll be on you like sharks on chum."

"Reality shows today, reality books tomorrow," Brunhilde said. "But Snoop Dogg's memoirs will sell better than a scoutmaster's, because Snoop has shot somebody."

"Ever shoot anyone, Charlie?" Nancy asked. They all laughed uproariously. I owned a gun. I wished it were here, now.

I slowed to give a logging truck room, and let them laugh. Striking out with five agents with one pitch had to be some sort of record. But Janet was awfully quiet. Perhaps she hadn't read my query, either, and I could start fresh with her tomorrow. First, I had to get them off of the topic of my book. "And Bread Pudding cookbooks? What about their future?"

As if she had heard my thoughts, Janet shook her head and sighed. "Cookbooks will be downloaded off the TV before too long. Thriller-memoirs and video games – that's all we'll have left. Creative fiction like yours will go the way of poetry."

Et tu, Janet, I might have said. Caesar, the sensitive, hopeful humanist lay bleeding, along with his dreams of enlightening the world through literature. But Cassius, the cowardly salesman, piped up, using my voice: "My book, *The History of the Universe* could easily be adapted as a video game."

The declaration cleared the air. "You're such a good sport, Charlie," Nancy said. "Send me fifty pages."

"Piker," Dick Rippington shot back. "I'll glance at the first one hundred without even seeing the query."

"Gosh, thanks." I grinned like a batter who just got a walk, but their invitations were really two strikes. This was the Game of the Writer's Conference. Big-leaguers sign baseballs, agents ask for chapters. Veterans know their submissions will never make it through the intern gauntlet.

Sy spoke confidentially, perhaps to spare my feelings. "Parapsychology? We can't sell stories full of that mumbo jumbo." Strike three. I wondered if Mrs. Sotheby would refund my discounted fee after I dropped these Cassandras off at the front door.

And then it happened – after a decade of futility and thirty minutes of rejection, we passed the four-thousand-foot mark and the Universe cleared its throat for a second time that day. A momentous blast of clairvoyance, a full-fledged vision seized my brain: In it, a frightened deer stood alone in the roadway ahead, around the next bend, still hidden from our view.

"I'm stopping," I cried out of desperation. Hell, I had nothing left to lose. "I just had a premonition there's a deer in the road, just around the next curve." I shot Sy a glance that said, *I'll show you mumbo jumbo.*

Their gasps were nothing compared to the uproar that ensued when we turned the corner and bore down on a twelve-point buck standing astraddle the yellow line.

"Hotcha," Sy said, eyes wide.

We screeched to a halt, but my psychic triumph was short-lived. After only a second, a greenish blur swept down from the road above and slammed the animal from behind, transforming the stately deer into a bag of bones that flew through the air and shattered my windshield with a thud. The creature hung there, one antler captured by a small hole it had gouged in the windshield. Yet it was yet alive, thrashing frantically, hooves scraping my van's new grill while the fifteen-year-old driving the truck that hit the poor creature made his getaway.

"My God," Sy said. Janet Stallings wept, but I could only think that my chance to land an agent had just been resurrected. If they couldn't sell paranormal before, perhaps they could now. I scrambled out to fetch a tire tool.

"You won't hurt it, will you?" Janet begged.

"Of course not." The agents braved the headliner to watch me hammer the windshield with the lug wrench

– the glass didn't shatter, but cracked just enough for the buck to jerk his fuzzy antler free. He swung his head viciously, missing me by inches. A cheer erupted, but turned to gasps as the deer staggered sideways, off the road, then right over the cliff.

"Stop," I yelled, watching my triumph turn to tragedy.

But Sy, sitting in his higher vantage point, waved excitedly. "No, Charlie –he's OK," he yelled.

"Save him, Charlie." Janet was a tearful Madonna peering through a cracked windshield. Had I found my agent?

I crept to the edge of the pavement, and leaned over. The shaking beast stood stranded on a small precipice below the road's shoulder. A nasty slide yawned to its left, but if I could coax it onto the negotiable path on the right – I was confident that the deer's survival would coerce all five passengers to read my novel. Or at least the first ten pages. I took a breath, and jumped.

But the granite outcropping crumbled when my boots landed. Down I plunged, followed by the poor buck in an avalanche of dirt, rocks and shrubbery – and screams. I hit my head and the sky twirled and blurred. The rest I heard in darkness: concerned agents' voices, a wailing ambulance, paramedics barking orders.

When finally my eyes opened, though, I beheld the buck, standing scraped and bleeding, its once sparkling eyes now docile and defeated. I lay on hard stone, not warm hospital sheets. I stretched, feeling my legs for breaks, breathing through aches and pains, until a snort turned me over. Not three feet away from my left foot stood the largest black bear I had ever seen. I blinked.

"Saints be praised, you're finally awake." A voice, mature, female – from nowhere. "Open your eyes and receive the gratitude of the forest." A massive tongue licked the huge black lips. I scanned around for the voice's owner, but the cramped rock cavern contained only me, the bear, and the bunged-up buck.

"Well?" A male voice, this time. The deer shuddered. "Aren't you going to answer Mama Bear?"

It was a dream, of course. I was surely safe in some hospital where they were simply over-juicing my morphine drip. "Nice bear," I said happily, waiting for the furry hallucination to dissolve. "I don't have anything to feed you. Go away, now --"

"Shut up," the female voice demanded at the same instant the bear reached out with one huge paw, and knocked me back against the rocks.

"That hurt," I cried. "Nurse! Someone get these animals out of my head."

But the animals didn't dissolve. Instead, the frightening bear lumbered closer, its eyes afire. My heart pounded, and I was about to scream when it stopped, its massive, wet snout only inches from my face. "Accept the gratitude of the forest and shut up," the female voice boomed, even as foul breath invaded my nose and mouth.

No. The voice seemed to coincide exactly with the glow in the monster's eyes.

"You?" I asked, and took another inventory, passing my hands all over my body. My beard was matted with something – blood? Was I dead? Or maybe I made it to the conference and my writer's club buddies slipped me a mickey. "Where's the hidden speaker? How could anyone talk to a bear?"

"You're psychic, aren't you?" The creature punctuated the question with a snarl. "That's all you could say in your sleep. How you ramble on – about how you can see things others can't, how you, alone, understand the universe's inner workings. Thank God that sniveling's over." Her massive shoulders blocked my view of the cave's entrance. "Forest protocol demands that any human who shows compassion be kept alive until properly thanked." She leered at the deer. "Well?"

"Yes, Mama Bear." Male voice again. "Thank you, human. You saved me." The deer's head dipped, a listless, insincere sort of bow, and never was a speech more laconic. The two forest beasts exchanged edgy looks. They were not friends.

"You're welcome," I said, determined the charade should stop. "You, too, Mama – Mama Bear. Can I call you that? Or is it Mrs. Bear – wait. What the hell am I saying?"

This was a hell of a drug flashback, and I had to gather my wits, I decided. I brushed my pants off one more time, and started to stand. If I didn't look at these hallucinations, they would fade away.

Or so I thought.

With a flick of a wide, heavy paw, Mama Bear reached out, tapped my shoulder, and sent me down again. My knees buckled, and my sore butt slammed flat onto the stone floor.

"Stop that," I cried. My heart raced wildly. This must be some sort of stroke or something. I started to whimper. "I've got a van of agents to transport," I said. "They must be waiting up on the road, so please excuse me--"

The black mass didn't move aside. "Your friends deserted you," she said.

"They did? When? How long was I unconscious?"

"I brought you both here yesterday."

I tried to scramble to my feet once more. This time, the bear let me. "Holy – Joke's over. I've missed almost the whole conference." Still the glare. No pranksters came laughing through the cave mouth. No animal trainers, not even a hunter with a gun. I blinked. Blinked again.

The cave was lit by sunlight from its small opening, but that light seemed to be fading. Whatever day it was, it must be nearing sunset. I dared another glance at those fiery black eyes, then checked the sad-looking, bleeding deer off in the corner.

The truth slowly oozed from the needle-prick pains in my knee, the iron taste of blood on my lips and a tangy stench of livestock: I had been knocked out, had somehow stumbled into a cave on the forest floor – these were real animals, and I was going through some psychic epiphany.

I realized: those visions earlier – they didn't mean I was going to get published at all. Instead, they must have been warning signs. Warning that the end was near. But, unlike other people who die, this wasn't my life flashing before my eyes, but some awful, twisted pageant. What karma was this? I even became a vegetarian a few years ago, so why was I picked out for a purgatory that included wounded mammals?

I started blubbering. "Please let me go. I have to get an agent."

Mama Bear huffed. "The nights grow cool and, as you can see, my larder is bare. Until you two happened down the mountain." A noble pose. "Humans have demon tongues, thus it is against our law to listen – for, like a flea-infested coyote, you will try to trick your way to freedom. But for this moment, I will disobey our laws, and grant you one more speech to calm my curiosity. Asleep, you said that word repeatedly. What is an *agent*?"

Her gaze was an inhuman window into a deep and terrifying cosmos that sucked me in. I might have wet my pants if I wasn't so dehydrated from the mountain air. These were wild animals – I wasn't afraid of the deer, for he seemed about to fall over. But that glimpse of – of – *nothing* – deep in the bear's eyes told me she could go postal at any moment.

"Well?"

"I'm a writer," I said, risking a baby step toward the cave entrance. "I need an agent so I can sell – uh, show my writing to the rest of – of humanity."

"What's a writer? Do you know, Bucky?" Mama Bear tossed her head, and peered over her shoulder at the deer. I grabbed my chance, and kept sliding silently along the wall.

Bucky answered plaintively, as if resigned to his fate. "Writers are humans who scratch little marks on papers. I see them all the time at Vernal Falls. They call it poetry and they seem quite taken with themselves when they are finished scratching."

"Marks, huh?" Daylight. Another step and I would be free – but Mama Bear turned, her body one huge, fluid, furry monolith, snatched me up off the ground, and draped me over her shoulder.

"This is it," I cried out.

But instead of sinking her teeth in, she bent down – still carrying me – and rumbled through the cave entrance, scraping my back against its jagged top in the process.

"Ow," I cried.

"Shut up, you sniveling excuse for a creature of God," her airborne voice boomed. "Here is writing – real writing." She grabbed my chin with a foul, musky paw, and shoved my face toward deep claw scrapes in the bark of a tree. "There. These scratches mean something. They mark where I bade farewell to my young one, Splinter, when he went off on his quest for male-ness."

I stared at the gouges, and my nose was pricked by the sweet smell of pine. If only she would put me down, I might have a chance at escape – But before I could finish my thought, she wheeled around, and plunged through the cramped hole, back into the stone prison, gripping me more firmly than ever.

She marched on the buck, and pinched my chin again, pushing me close to the deer. "Show him more writing, Bucky," she demanded.

The condemned deer turned slowly, giving me a clear view of the deep, bloody crevices on his left flank. This was like a drug trip gone bad. "That's not writing," I wailed between sobs. "Humans don't write to destroy things. We use our marks to tell stories."

The bear's jaw fell open. "Scratches on paper aren't stories. I won't let you die without reading a real story." She put a weighty paw on either side of my face, looked into my eyes, and squeezed. My heart cramped. Once again, my being concluded: *This is it!*

Before I could scream or make peace with God, or even focus on the sort of life I wished for when I was next reincarnated, a scene exploded in my brain: a three-D sort of movie starring a mountain lion who snatched a baby bear from a trail. The cat trotted off with its prize, but a mother bear leaped from the bush at the last moment, tossed the lion high into the air, and when it came down, the mother bear committed atrocities I didn't think possible.

Another scene – I could actually taste the crisp air, feel the brambles on my skin – rabbits, raccoons, and other creatures lay parched beneath a blazing sun. Mama Bear – it looked like her – came from nowhere and kicked over a huge stone, loosing a gush of water underneath. The animals struggled forward to drink.

Another bear cub came into view – this tyke secured in a cage carried by two scroungy men. Mama Bear dropped from a tree and took them both down before they fired a shot.

Release. I fell back, hitting my head again. The bear hovered, letting ultimate humiliation sink in. Compared to the smells, the feels, the rushes of blood and true feeling that her tales conjured, my feeble little plots were nothing.

She drew closer, and this time my own wretched life finally passed before me: Eight years waiting tables and selling mushrooms to put Christina through med school. The pot bust for which she wouldn't take the blame. Well, it was my pot. But I was a writer. At first, Christina admired that, but her love dissipated in direct proportion to my mounting rejection slips. "You're writing about life instead of living it," she always said. She was right, I realized in that agonizing instant, and the hot bear breath descending around me told me it was too late to change my stripes now.

"I'm unworthy," I cried. "Your stories are better than Vonnegut, Hesse – even John Grisham. Are they all true?"

"Of course they're true." Flaring nostrils. "What idiot would tell stories he doesn't know anything about?"

"I do it all the time," I screamed, then remembered myself. "But landing an agent with your stories would be a slam-dunk."

A deep grunt. "Agents again. What are these agents?"

"In my van." I waved, hopeless now. "Any one of them could get you seven figures."

She reared, and I braced for the end, but she only surveyed the cave, her larder. Again Bucky was her resource. "How many agents in the van?"

The deer answered wearily. "A bunch. Couldn't count them all, because I was in shock, and there was some weird yellow moss hanging from the vehicle's ceiling."

"You saw them?" I fumed. "Why did they leave me?"

Bucky actually shrugged. "From the bottom of the hill, it was hard to hear their speech, but I think the fey one said something about missing cocktail hour, and they drove off."

Sharp claws probed my ribs, and something about the glint in the bear's eye sparked unexpected hope: perhaps I didn't have enough meat on my bones to last her the entire winter. Who said bulimia was all bad? Still, I acted dejected. "I could have introduced you to them." I sighed. "With a best-seller you could've had a bigger cave, or filled this one with acorns." I almost managed a tear. "Even mushrooms."

She scraped a single claw across my temple, and my heart stopped. "Get me an agent," she growled.

We climbed the steep mountain in gathering darkness – and shame, not victory. Could the sleek monster rumbling behind me be trusted? Or had I saved myself and Bucky only to sacrifice my writer friends and the agents I coveted? "Stay calm," I begged her repeatedly. "We're after a book deal, not fast food, understand?" Her bear sneer didn't reassure.

I felt in my pocket for the hotel key card Mrs. Sotheby had given me yesterday. If the bear misbehaved, I would alert the others, dart to my room and lock the door. Bucky read my thoughts again, and hobbled alongside. "Don't even think about it," he said. "A bear can outrun even me over short distances."

Stars broke over the mountain's crest, and the air filled with laughter. The final conference cocktail party was obviously in full swing. A paw fell heavily on my back. "No tricks, Writer," Mama Bear said. "Point out the Alpha Agent, the stag, the He-Bear. I'll do the rest." Licking her chops. "And don't fret about your precious friends. Man is the only creature that kills more than he intends to eat." My stomach convulsed as we emerged from the thick ferns.

"Ahoy, It's Charlie-boy," Dick Rippington shouted in his Oxford accent. "And see what he has brought us. Bravo." The corporate-casually dressed writers, obviously already deep in their cups, spilled from the ground-floor hospitality suite onto the lawn. Rather than flinch as the beasts lumbered closer, they raised glasses in impromptu toasts. Dick threw his arm around me. "This giant Kodiak will make a better story than the marmot that nibbled my bum in the hedgerow last night."

Rather than warn him, I steamed. "Why the hell did you leave me?"

"What? Stay and prevent the consummate mountain man from rescuing wildlife?" A salute. "Well done."

I should have screamed bloody murder, but both animals seemed suddenly dumb and harmless, sniffing among the hoard of writers like cowed dogs. For an instant, I wondered if I imagined the whole episode. Authors swarmed Bucky. "Oh, you darling thing, you're hurt," Brunhilde said.

Mrs. Sotheby used her clipboard to push Dr. Morten, a fellow student in our writing club for the last ten years – mysteries – forward. "There's anti-biotic in the side suite," she said.

"Certainly." Morten hustled to do his Hippocratic duty. Brunhilde and Nancy led the deer through the crowd, but I watched Mama Bear turn her nose up at the cold-cuts tray. Not a good sign. By the time I crossed the room, she already had Sy wrapped in a hug.

"Sy, this is--"

But she was staring into his eyes, braced in her story-telling pose, with her broad arm around his shoulders. Sy gasped. "Impossible," he said, no doubt captivated by a telepathic movie similar to the one she had showed me.

"This is Mama Bear, Sy."

He nodded, but did not break her gaze. "She just introduced herself." Her nose twitched, angling toward the cocktail fast in his hand, and he offered a sip. "Mama, thanks for taking care of our boy, here. He's psychic, you know."

Mama Bear replied with telepathy I could not make out. Sy laughed. I had to keep them on the right track. "Sy, Mama Bear has some stories--"

"Yeah, yeah." He handed me his empty glass. "Why don't you run along, Sonny, and let the pros talk?" To Mama: "Come to my room and you can show me your etchings." Definitely the very wrong thing to say to her.

The sea parted so the giants could pass, and the furry one shot me a look. I started to scream a warning when Dick nudged me. "Good old Sy. Gets lucky about twice a year," he whispered. "Why else would a demigod bang around these cheesy conferences?"

"I have to stop them," I blurted, possessed of a deep sense of right and wrong, maybe for the first time in my life. At that instant, nothing on earth could have

stopped me from following them, even sacrificing myself
to save that dear old literary guru, except for the sight I
saw in the corner: Janet Stallings, alone on the hospitality
room couch. I scrambled to her side.

"Charlie. Ooh, that's a nasty cut on your head."

"Never mind," I said. "I've missed the whole
conference. Would you consider representing my novel?"

"I'm afraid of those animals," she said, eyes
lowered. "But I prefer whole manuscripts to pitch
sheets."

"I've got the book in my suitcase."

A weak smile. "Walk me to my room and we'll
pick it up on the way. I can't stand these parties."

My blood boiled at the possibilities. Sy was a big
boy, and the beast didn't seem that hungry. Like any she-
animal, Janet wanted me on her own turf. I was
tantalized, and emerged from my own room with the
manuscript in both hands.

"My, that's a big one," she said.

"Eleven hundred pages. My style's a lot like
Michener's," I said. In her room, I laid the book on her
bed. "Should I stick around to answer questions while
you read?" I was too excited to come up with a better
line.

"No, Charlie. But thanks for rescuing the deer. You
are brave, and I expect a lot from this manuscript." She
opened her patio door and pushed me out into the night
with a shove that belied her petite-ness.

Dick Rippington and a handful of supplicants
were back out on the lawn's edge, peering into the forest.

Alarm bells. "Oh, no," I yelled. "Did the bear take Sy down there?"

"Ssh," Dick said. "You'll scare the marmots."

In the hospitality suite, Brunhilde and Nancy were hanging bagels from Bucky's antlers like god-awful Christmas ornaments.

"This could never happen in New *Yawk*," Brunhilde said.

Nancy beamed. "Charlie, Brunny had a great idea – a coffee table cookbook with endangered animals modeling the recipes. Presentation is half of gourmet cooking, anyway."

"We'll go halfsies on representation and distribute through the Sierra Club," Brunhilde said brightly.

Bucky's eyes swam as he leaned his head close to mine. "Run while you still can," he said.

I did, straight to my room, fantasizing about Janet, snug in her bed, reading my work. I successfully shut out thoughts of Sy, and curled up in the darkness in my hotel bed – so much more comfy than a cave floor.

Then the screams started. Raw, human, pitiful yelps of pain, echoing through the tall pines, through the mountain hollows, fairly rattling the windows of my room.

The utter horror of what I had done sent me deeper under the covers. Mama Bear weighed a good five hundred pounds, and Sy was every bit as slight as that poor mountain lion she decimated in her story.

My career was over before it started. Any author even associated with the conference that killed Sy Nanderjack would surely be blackballed. He was an institution, and I was accomplice to his murder. When this got out, and the talented writers in my club – my last friends on earth – realized I was responsible for this atrocity, we would be friends no more. I lay there, shivering with each scream – I should have just taken my medicine in Mama Bear's cave.

I woke early, and brushed my teeth, wondering what toothpaste they issue in jail. Writers sleep in on the last day of a conference, so escape might still be possible. But surely the police were already here, and tracking my van – with its windshield broken from the collision – would be all too easy for the cops.

In the lobby, no blue uniforms, only Mrs. Sotheby, with hangover hair, directing the packing-up of display tables. "Charlie," she said, pointing. "Go tell that stuffed-shirt you can't smoke in public in California."

I slogged across the stone floor and my heart stopped. Sy Nanderjack reclined solo in one of the plush armchairs in front of the hotel's giant fireplace, lighting his own fire to a bulky Meerschaum.

"You – you're all right," I sputtered. "But I heard screams."

"Yeah?" A smile. "Probably the all-night poetry reading. They were re-enacting Ginsberg's first performance of *Howl*." He stood up. "When does your van leave for the airport?"

I checked my watch – broken crystal, but still running. "Uh, thirty minutes," I said. "I guess."

He stretched and yawned. A tap of his foot made me look down: I was standing in the lush fur of the largest bearskin rug I had ever seen. Flat and tanned, its huge head aimed at the gift shop. I stepped off. Big brown eyes – blank, but unmistakably familiar, and beside a back leg, a fresh pool of blood.

I gagged. "No. It can't be her," I cried.

"Oh, no?" He puffed on the pipe. "Some writers just don't take rejection as well as you do, Charlie-boy."

I stood, catatonic, as he winked insipidly, and sauntered off, puffing pipe clouds toward the vaulted ceiling. I knelt in front of poor Mama Bear's flattened body. I wanted to cradle that massive head and beg forgiveness, but clouds shifted in the vaulted windows above, casting tree shadows down over me. A glance up. The shadows fell not from tree branches, but the antlers of a deer head mounted fifteen feet above the fireplace. Bucky. There was no mistaking him, his noble neck bore so many scratches and gashes. And the real proof: a single bagel still hung from one of the horns.

Nancy and Brunhilde emerged, laughing, from the coffee shop, each clutching a breakfast sandwich. "There's our boy," Brunhilde said between munches. A pungent odor pricked my nostrils. "We'll get our bags."

Nancy offered a bite of hers. "This place makes the best Venison McBagels I've ever tasted."

I declined and escaped into the brisk morning air to keep from barfing. Dick Rippington was gingerly climbing into the van's middle seat. "I say, do you have a pillow?" he asked.

"Afraid not." The keys were in the ignition.

"Hope you don't mind." He ripped down a handful of the sagging headliner, fashioned it into a foam cushion of sorts, and sat on it. "Ah. Much better," he said. "Bloody marmots."

Through the cracked windshield, I saw Janet Stallings rolling her bag straight for me. Here came the River card. "Morning, Charlie." She parked the luggage. I hopped out.

"Hi, Janet. Well, what do you think?"

A blank look.

"My novel. Did you like it?"

"Oh, that." Her face turned crimson. "Sorry, Charlie. It was so late, and I made the mistake of picking up the phone book and reading that for a while. You have such funny street names out here. Like *Minnewawa*."

A laugh, but she read my face. "Tell you what." Pensive hands folded together. "They'll never allow something that heavy on the plane, so I left your manuscript in the room. Send me a query in about six weeks, 'K? I'm drowning in slush just now."

She took her place next to Dick. "Minnewawa?" he said. "Sounds Welsh." They laughed together.

I fetched new water bottles from the lobby and loaded the bags. Writers waved goodbye. Tears. Laughter. I drove downhill slowly, enduring the cracked windshield and the void Janet had planted in my belly.

Then, as we neared Lawson's Grade, the Universe made one last belch. Another epiphanic voice from nowhere told me Janet really had read the book, and wanted to represent. Further, the vision insisted, she had ordered a contract prepared, and would spring the surprise on me before we reached the airport. Why did these infernal astral messages keep insisting I would be published, when it was painfully obvious that would never happen?

I turned the vehicle downward, onto the steep grade, still awash in this fresh vision, when Sy tensed.

"What's that?" he said, peering out the window.

A deafening roar enveloped us. Ahead, a helicopter descended from above the mountain peaks, toward the grade, and bizarrely, a windblown lass in a tasteful business suit hung from a ladder below the chopper, clutching a sheaf of papers. Janet leaned up between the front seats, and tapped my shoulder.

"That's Melissa, from my San Francisco office," she cried. "I lied, Charlie. I did read your book, and loved it. Called her at two this morning and told her to get on a plane. She must have barely missed us at the hotel. Pull over." Janet was bouncing on the seat with excitement. "Pull over, I said. They're landing, and Melissa's got your contract."

It was my latest vision, come alive. All breath left my body. A dream – my dream of being a novelist – was coming true at last – but wait!

"Are you sure, Janet?" I said, keeping it polite. "I dropped you at your room at nine. You read all eleven hundred pages between then and two o'clock?"

"No, silly." She smiled demurely, and the others broke out with knowing chuckles. "I meant two o'clock New York time. It was eleven here when I finished."

The copter eased toward us, but I was still moving, slow-go in low gear. My voice rose. "You read over a thousand pages in two hours?"

"Oh, be serious, Charles, my boy," Dick yelled. "She knows a good thing without reading all of it."

"That's right," Janet said, her smile larger than ever. "I had only to read the first chapter to know I was in love with it." A meaningful wink. I wanted so much to believe in that wink.

I returned her smile, took the next curve, and scanned the other agents in the rear-view mirror. These clowns had deserted me before – were they actually going to admit me into their club now? After all these years of rejection?

"But the first chapter is one hundred and ninety-three pages," I protested.

Janet leaned forward again. Very close. "I'm a speed reader, my love." The thudding blades of the helicopter dropped toward the steep highway.

My mouth fell open. This was for real. I tried to form the words, warn everyone that I was stopping the van in the turnout up ahead, but Sy interrupted.

"Y'know, Charlie, you're a damned good chauffeur. My suggestion, if you really want to make the big bucks, is forget this novel-writing jazz and start your own limo service."

I looked at Janet. So beautiful. Industrious and oh, so professional.

Then again, what if I was letting sexual urges get in the way of my real ambitions?

Mrs. Sotheby always said – hell, *everybody* always said – that a smart writer looks for the most experienced, the most successful agent. And here he was – the wisest sage of the New York publishing scene, King Nanderjack himself – offering free advice to me. Me, a humble, unpublished writer. Who was I to ignore these golden crumbs of insight – crumbs that would lead to certain success – thrown down by an opinion-maker of his stature?

I kept driving.

THE END

About the Author...

Bull Marquette is the penname for a Texas native who began his writing career as an ad and book jacket writer for Word Books, a religious book publisher, where he was privileged to interview notables like Jeb Magruder – refugee from President Nixon's Watergate scandal, and 1960s civil rights activist Eldridge Cleaver, as well as authors who had come back from the dead.

He has also worked as an ad agency copywriter, convenience store clerk, high school teacher, construction worker, TV weatherman, radio announcer, apprentice cook under a world-class chef, waiter, bread delivery man, speech writer for a state legislator, branch manager for a national stock brokerage firm and financial advisor. Bull moved to California in 1982 to study parapsychology in the unique masters program at JFK University.

He served as business editor of THE FRESNO WEEKLY newspaper for two years, where he also wrote a humorous editorial column and articles on world events, including "Psychics Who Work with Police Departments" and the events after 9/11.

Bull co-hosted the nationally syndicated WEBMASTER RADIO SHOW, an interview show that featured the giants of the high tech world during the climax of the Dot-Com bubble, from February 2000 to November 2001. He is currently a financial advisor, a columnist for THE FRESNO BEE, and a sometimes announcer for KVPR, national public radio in Fresno.

A paranormal and "alternate history" buff, Bull is marketing his debut novel, THE FIFTH PLANE, an exciting story of terrorism in America that starts the day after 9/11. He has written several more novels and a number of short stories.

www.ingramcontent.com/pod-product-compliance
Lightning Source LLC
Chambersburg PA
CBHW050929120626
46552CB00001B/109

* 9 7 8 0 9 8 2 0 4 7 4 1 5 *